The Story of the Rosary

The Story
of the
Rosary

Anne Vail

PASSIO CHRISTI CONFORTA ME

The Neumann Press
Long Prairie, Minnesota 56347

CONTENTS

Introduction 7
Chapter One 11
Chapter Two 33
Chapter Three 57
Chapter Four 75
Chapter Five 93
Chapter Six 113
Selection of Primary Sources 153
Notes 155

Meditations on the Mysteries

The Joyful Mysteries 123
The Sorrowful Mysteries 132
The Glorious Mysteries 143

Illustrations

The Virgin at the Fountain 10
Caxton's Print of Chaucer 32
St. Dominic 56
The Rosary of King Henry VIII 74
The Battle of Lepanto 92
Polish Pilgrim with Rosary 112

For

Dominic, Joanna and Thomas

INTRODUCTION

THE Rosary occupies a unique place in the life of a Catholic, and for centuries has probably been the prayer which is most loved and used outside the liturgy. This book is also unique, for it combines a carefully researched history of the Rosary—which in parts is almost a history of the Church itself—with an inspiring love of the Rosary as a devotion. This is helped by an excellent series of meditations on the fifteen mysteries at the end.

It is often said that the health of the Church can be gauged by the state of devotion to Our Lady. When that devotion is fervent and firmly based on the teachings and approved practices of the Church, then the health of Catholicism will be good. If Our Lady is neglected, or her cult distorted by superstitious beliefs and practices, then the Church itself in that age or country will be in a bad state.

In our own day there has been a sad decline in devotion to Mary, in extreme cases amounting to contempt for the veneration given to her on account of her unique privileges and merits as the Mother of God. This book should do much to reverse that decline, and bring back to the prayer of the rosary those who, probably through inadvertence, have ceased to use it. It will help others as well. There have always been Catholics who found the rosary difficult because of the repetitive nature of the prayers themselves and its *unintellectual* character. This book will show how it is a useful aid to meditating on the principle events in the life of Christ and His Mother. It will help young Catholics who may never really have been taught about the use of the rosary at all, and will be of great assistance to all those who use the rosary regularly and wish to deepen their prayer.

Rev. Dr. T. C. G. Glover, M.A., J.C.D.

CHAPTER ONE

The story told by the rosary
Is the story of primitive beauty,
True as the burden of folk-songs
It is a song piped on the hills
By a shepherd calling his sheep.

From: *The Rosary* by Caryll Houselander

THE VIRGIN AT THE FOUNTAIN by Jan Van Eyck — *Koninklijk Museum voor Schone Kunsten Antwerpen.*

CHAPTER ONE

THE word rosary has two meanings and at first glance there seems little connection between them.

Until the twelfth-century any Englishman would have staked if not his life, at least his hat, on the knowledge that a rosary or roserie was an enclosed garden for roses. Even today some horticulturalists will insist that a roserie is the correct term for such an area in the same way as they would describe an arboretum for trees. The mere suggestion of roses and enclosed gardens conveys an air of mystery and delight, for the rose is the acknowledged favourite of the flower garden and conjures up images of secret gardens, of Alice in Wonderland stumbling into the giant rose garden. For most Englishmen there is the knowledge that the rose had for centuries been the emblem of their country, long before the Tudors adopted the rose for their own.

During the latter part of the twelfth-century strange things happened to the word rosary and a different meaning crept into the language. A small circlet of beads carried by clergy and laity alike, bearing no similarity to a rose, but given the name, at first by country people, gradually becoming universal in that strange way that customs have, until a Dominican monk named Thomas de Cintempre formally acknowledged this title by chance remark in the thirteenth-century.

At first glance that is what appears to have happened. By stretching the imagination and gathering convenient comparisons between the shape of flower garlands and circles of beads, the shift in meaning becomes obvious. As the popularity of this new form of prayer spread throughout Europe in the following centuries, the original meaning of the word was gradually lost and today the term rosary is everywhere accepted as the name given to beads of prayer and any connection with roses or rose gardens has for the most part been discarded.

The choice seems almost haphazard and is difficult to accept without question, for it seems unlikely that by chance or happy accident prayer beads should have been given this romantic name which was then to survive to the present day, some seven centuries later. In any case, the connection between flower garlands and rosaries was tenuous. Apart from any other consideration, prayer beads were rarely made in the form of a circle, but were left to hang straight until someone had the happy notion of looping the ends together to form a ring. My own curiosity about the subject might have ended there but for a recent experience in Italy which began a long journey of discovery into the history of the rosary, in an effort to find the true connection, if there be one, between these two apparently different meanings.

I was visiting Florence in early September just before the arrival of Autumn, and the heat of late Summer hung over the city. Mid-afternoon is the time for visitors because those in the know have escaped to their siestas. The newcomer is left momentarily startled at his good luck and judgement at setting out at a time when the city appears to be empty, leaving him to gaze undisturbed on the river as it curls around the city beneath graceful bridges, before winding on in a sparkled haze through Tuscany. Then turning from such pleasant manderings, guide book in hand, the tourist sets off in search of the Duomo.

In an attempt to find shade, I leant on a small wooden door and found myself in the Church of the Annunciation, momentarily blinded by the darkness and shocked by the silence as the roar of traffic was sliced by the door swinging closed behind me. Gradually my eyes grew accustomed to the gloom and I was able to see kneeling figures, beads in hand, casting long shadows on the wall beyond. In the suffused light, I could see above the figures a panel displaying a pillar of roses with the words *Rosa Mystica* written in clear relief below.

There were only a dozen or so women, clad in black, and in the cool air time seemed suspended, revealing a scene from a bygone age forgotten and overlooked by the world that roared past beyond the cloisters. The sight before me was so familiar that it scarcely registered on my preoccupied mind, and yet something caused me to stop and with a growing awareness, almost of shock, I realised that months, perhaps years, had passed since I had last heard that familiar prayer, a soft murmuring without inflection. Somehow it had seemed safe to presume that while time fled past, in the darkened lady chapels of hallowed churches there were still those devout souls fingering their beads, and in their rhythmic devotion lay the promise of sanity in a confused world. It seemed inconceivable that such age old customs should cease.

I tried to remember when I had last tiptoed past such a gathering, or perhaps clumsily knelt in its midst, always aware that impatience and worldliness must shriek amongst the quiet holiness. I found it impossible to recall such an occasion in recent memory, and the cause of the strange new silence in "architect-designed" churches became painfully clear. While there are enthusiastic revivals in some places, for most the prayer of the rosary is an anachronism and an eerie stillness has fallen in Catholic churches.

I knew that it had not always been so. There was a time when jewels fit for a king's ransome hung in decades of ten; when a Spanish noblewoman and saint announced her presence with the scent of dried roses encased in beads, when the kettledrums of war all but crushed swords cast with rosary rings. In more peaceful times garlands of flowers in May gladdened the heart of a pilgrim king and the rose of England proclaimed her to be the dowry of the Mother of God; there were occasions when the prayer of the rosary was heard and the course of history was altered. And all for a small circlet of beads that took nearly a thousand years to develop into the prayer we know today as the rosary, eagerly grasped by some and even more eagerly cast aside by others. An optional extra in the paraphernalia on offer from the Catholic Church, held on to steadfastly by some unwilling or unable to explain their reasons to others too impatient to stop and listen, until gradually any understanding of the meaning of the rosary becomes lost. When that understanding has been lost, there will be many to deny there was ever any meaning in the first place.

The devotion of those elderly women for their rosaries can be mystifying to those who have no knowledge of its history. Yet those same women would probably be unaware that such a story existed and would find any explanation quite unnecessary. In a sense, they can be forgiven for it is essentially a prayer of our own time with such powers of meditation that would make a guru groan with envy. Unlike peddlars of twentieth century-meditation who advocate long hours of introspection, the meditation of the mysteries of the rosary involves the total withdrawal from self to a state of peace from which true development of the spiritual life of the soul begins.

The Oxford Dictionary defines a rosary as a rose garden and as a form of devotion in which five or fifteen decades of Aves are repeated, each decade preceded by a Paternoster, and followed by the Gloria. For the sake of definition this is a neat distinction but as that mysterious panel displaying roses in the Church of the Annunciation hinted, the rose as a symbol is a vital part of the rosary. The two images overlap like a tapestry whose different threads, meaningless on their own, gradually come together to form a picture.

Those Italian women praying in the shadows of the Church of the Annunciation beneath the words *Rosa Mystica* could find themselves as easily at the end of this story, for all the information gained on the way can only result in the knowledge that it is the perfect prayer offered through the Mother of God to her Son. In the cool of that church all the threads are drawn together, for the *Mystical Rose* is an epithet of Our Lady from the Litany of Loretto and the prayer of the rosary is her especial prayer.

*   *   *   *   *   *   *

"And the Lord God had planted a paradise of pleasure from the beginning; wherein He placed man whom He had formed."[1] There can be few words that cast a more vivid impression of the importance of gardens to the early Christians. From the very beginning man sought by his labours to recreate the beauties of the Garden of Eden, as if to rediscover the time of peace when he walked with God in the cool of the evening, and in the happiness of Paradise lay the beginnings of the story of the rosary.

So much has been written about Paradise and yet we are as far as ever from any precise understanding. The actual site of the Garden of Eden occupied the imagination of researchers and hopeful travellers throughout the early centuries who searched in vain for an earthly Paradise. On some mediaeval maps, the Garden is shown on the plains edging the great Euphrates river, not far from the spot on which Nebuchadnezzar planted the Hanging Gardens of Babylon for his homesick bride from the mountains. In the fourteenth-century, Sir John Mandeville confidently explained to his wondering readers that the Garden of Eden was perched on a mountain of such immense height that as the moon moved through the heavens, her skirt trailed across its velvet lawns. Although there were undoubtedly differing opinions as to the existence of the Garden of Eden, either in a material or spiritual form, it was the latter which became the accepted view of the Church. To the writers of the Old Testament however the existence of Paradise was beyond question in both senses.

From the practical point of view, the ideal garden figures as the earliest home of the human race, a place for the souls of the blessed in the traditions of nearly all the ancient nations. A place of such mystical beauty that it is set deep within the nature of man to mourn the loss and to yearn for rediscovery, for the union of the Creator with His created is the sublime, and yet at the same time, most natural state of affairs.

The words of Genesis have captured man's imagination throughout the ages and the description of the Garden of Eden is at once awesome and beautiful. Because geographically the Hebrew writers lived in an area of heat and drought, and also because of their veneration of "high places", great importance was given to various elements of the Paradise Garden.

In the accounts of Genesis, the Tree of Knowledge dominates all else, creating at the same time the second element of shade, and with it the suggestion of peace and respite from the relentless heat. In the same book we learn that God Himself "in the cool of the day" walked in the shade of the trees He had planted, an image created by the words, "They heard the voice of the Lord God walking in Paradise at the cool of the day"[2] is full of wonder.

The third and equally important element of the Paradise Garden was water. In a terrain of such wilderness, where little or no rain fell for six months of the year, the gardens of Palestine, like those of Egypt and Persia, were a network of elaborately arranged waterways.

In the early Persian gardens, the central feature was a large water-tank placed at such an angle that the water gently over-flowed to irrigate the garden which was carefully divided into four parts as in the Garden of Eden.

Isaiah uses the imagery of a watered garden with great beauty: "and the Lord will give thee rest continually and will fill thy soul with brightness and deliver thy bones; and thou shalt be like a watered garden and like a fountain of water whose waters shall not fail."[3] To the people of Egypt, few words could have been more eloquent.

In the Song of Solomon, said to be the most beautiful and sen-suous poem ever written, the truly spiritual nature of the Old Testament is most vividly portrayed and it has been a source of joy and sanctity to some of the greatest saints of the Church. This was the favourite text of St. Bernard of Clairvaux, and St. Thomas Aquinas is reputed to have died with the words of the Song on his lips.

To be understood on different levels as a means of unravelling layers of secrecy, the Song in lyric terms describes the awakening garden of Spring in which the lover greets the beloved, the young Christian Church anticipates the City of God, and all may feel the joy of grace entering the soul.

For the Song prefigures the Blessed Virgin Mary, and the garden is the symbol of the Beloved of Christ with apt allusion to the treasure of water. "My sister, my spouse is a garden enclosed, a fountain sealed up."[4]

In poetic terms an exiled people were to learn of the coming of the new Eve, from whose inviolate womb would emerge the

Christ Child to lead man back to Paradise, and that holy womb became the garden enclosing all heaven and earth, transforming all that had gone before.

In the early litanies, Our Lady is referred to as the "hortens conclusus" the enclosed garden, and it was a theme that was to be taken up and developed over the centuries.

An early representation of the "Enclosed Garden" is to be found in the Grimany Breviary in the library of St. Marks Cathedral in Venice. Based on the mystic references from the Canticles and Ecclesiasticus, the artist depicts a small garden "enclosed" in the centre of which is the "fountain of living water" surrounded by the rose of Sharon and by lilies. Above the castle of the "City of God" there shines the Stella Maris and in the fields beyond stands an olive tree beside the great cedar of Lebanon. In the foreground an angel holds the "mirror of purity".

The subject of the enclosed garden was much loved by painters of the Middle Ages who, with exquisite care, illustrated this profound mystery to a people, unable in most cases to read or write, but who were accustomed by means of intricate symbolism to "read" the picture placed before them.

One of the most famous of these pictures is called the "Paradise Garden" sometimes known as the "Mary Garden", painted by an unknown Flemish artist of the fifteenth-century. The enclosed garden symbolised the Virgin birth taken from the words of the Song of Solomon. Mary the Queen of Heaven is seated upon a cushion reading while her Child plays on the ground beside her, His Royal lineage from the House of David suggested by the iris. The purity of Our Lady is indicated by the white lilies while the red roses symbolising divine love grow beneath the cherry tree on the left, the cherries in turn aptly representing the joys of heaven. The water trough was said to associate the Blessed Virgin with the "well of living waters" and the lilies of the valley in the foreground denote both her meekness and purity.[5] All these observations are made for us by two writers of the later Middle Ages, Petrus Crescentius and Giovanni Boccaccio.[6]

As water was looked upon as a treasure beyond compare and the source of life in that parched land, so the words of the Song "like a fountain enclosed" were an inspiration to painters. In the "Virgin of the Fountain" painted by Jan van Eyck in the fifteenth-century, Our Lady is portrayed with the Infant Jesus beside the symbolic fountain and the Child trails a rosary on one small finger.

The association of Our Lady with the "enclosed garden" was established therefore from the earliest writings. Imperceptibly those gardens became rose gardens and as the idea took hold, so the painters almost smothered their pictures of the Blessed Virgin with roses, as trellises, trees and frequently clouds of petals surrounded. her image.

In the "Virgin of the Rose Garden" by Stefano da Zevio, Our Lady is seated with the Holy Child on her lap beside a sparkling fountain in the garden enclosed by an exotic trellis of roses with birds and angels perched precariously amongst the leaves and in the foreground St. Catherine is weaving a garland of roses.[7] According to a legend from the Middle Ages there was a youth to whom Our Lady appeared whilst he recited his Aves. As each prayer left his lips, she gathered it in her hands and it became a rose. Of these Our Lady wove a crown and placed it on her head.[8]

The moment at which the rose became Our Lady's especial emblem is more difficult to trace. From the time of Greek mythology the rose had been a symbol of pagan love and was therefore viewed with deep suspicion by the Church.

The Egyptians did little to further the cause of the rose. Guests of Anthony and Cleopatra had to wade through eighteen inches of rose petals strewn in their honour, and Emperor Heliogabhus entertained his guests by releasing huge quantities of petals from the ceiling of his banqueting hall, and as the record calmly states "they all died", from suffocation. Even amidst these strange events, there were hints of a more auspicious future. Unable to grow sufficient plants themselves, the Egyptians arranged for exotic cargoes of rose petals to be carried from an island in the Mediterranean which they named Rhodes, from the Greek "rhodan" for rose. The island of Rhodes later became renowned as the home of the Knights of Malta who played an important part in the story of the rosary.

The Egyptians were not alone in their preoccupation with roses. From the Tuscan hills of Italy, cooled by breezes from the Appenines, Pliny made detailed lists of his favourite roses, a happy pastime for any gardener, and it was his uncle whom curiosity served so cruelly when he travelled to view the erupting Vesuvius.

These lists written with loving care by Pliny go some way to explaining which varieties were growing at the time. From frescoes found in Pompeii there is evidence that the damask rose flourished there, and centuries later this rose was brought to Europe by Thibault le Chansonnier on his return from the valley of Damascus after the fourth Crusade. Unlike the modern rose which could hardly find itself the subject of such attention, with its monotonous flowering season and lack of scent, the rose seen by the early Christian was undoubtedly the Damask rose, whose flowers of delicious fragrance are born on graceful arching stems. The rose of Provins and the rosa Sancta are both of equal antiquity. The latter is often known as the Holy Rose for its five petals were said to represent the five wounds of Christ.

Gradually the increasing use of roses could no longer be ignored by the Church. While some searched anxiously for suitable sources of reference, others unclouded by intellectual ramifications, showed a deeper understanding of their faith and saw beyond the pagan vanities to a vision of creation, recognising all beauty as a reflection of the Creator.

Nowhere was this more evident than in pagan Rome itself. Perhaps the ceaseless tramp to and fro of the Roman Legions was prompted by the need for huge displays of strength, as if opulence might be synonomous with permanence. On many of these occasions citizens of importance and other dignitaries wore crowns of roses as a sign of victory, but whispers of a different God were abroad and this custom was adopted by Christian martyrs on their way to die for love of a King whose crown was made of thorns.

"Let us crown ourselves with rose-buds" says the book of

Wisdom and in the Middle Ages garlands became a sign of heavenly joy.

Centuries later when the word "garland" or "chapelet" became used as the name of Our Lady's beads, some of the Church authorities were to object strongly on the grounds that it was worldly, insisting that in its stead, the title "Our Lady's Psalter" be used. Perhaps they had overlooked the origin of these garlands, but no-one seems to have taken much notice and the name continued to be used, indeed to this day the title given to rosary beads in German is rosenkranz, crown of roses.

Although on special occasions, the wearing of a garland continued to be a sign of unusual importance, such considerations were happily ignored on most days of festival and they were worn by all. In England Whit Sunday was often known as Rose Sunday, and with garlands woven from the briar rose of the hedgerows, known by children as "Sweet Maria", processions wound their way down the lanes of every village in the month of May which is traditionally the month of Mary.

In his Canterbury Tales when describing the travels of the pilgrims on their way to the tomb of St. Thomas à Becket, Chaucer wrote:

> "Thou with they gerland, wrough of rose and lilie,
> Thee, mene I maid and martir, St. Cecilie."

This was a reference to the legend of St. Cecelia in which an angel gave her a crown of roses foretelling her martrydom.

The rose season was shorter than today for this was long before the era of the "perpetual flowering" varieties and thus the rose growers worked feverishly to fulfill their orders for garlands. Even the clergy produced roses on these occasions and a proscribed area of the abbey garden was set aside for roses to be grown by the priests not for the altars alone, but to provide sufficient blooms for their garlands. This part of the monastic garden was called a roserie and it must have been an idyllic spot, "for nothing liken me more, than dwelling by the roser eye . . ."

exclaimed Chaucer. No wastage was allowed, for as the garlands were woven into shape, the petals that fell from industrious hands were often scattered on the abbey floor, in honour of the Holy Spirit.

In Paris, the Chapelliers de fleurs was the only trade guild given special permission to work on Sundays during the season to compete with the huge demand for roses. A note of caution was sounded amidst the euphoria however by St. Louis King of France, who in memory of the crucifixion, forbade his sons to wear rose garlands on a Friday.

As an echo of the words of the song: "A garden enclosed is my sister, my bride, a spring shut up, a fountain sealed", the word rose implies a mystery and as if to emphasise this, they are often grown apart in secluded areas of their own. There is an expression "under the rose" which is used to suggest discretion and in the Middle Ages, the rose itself was often used as a sign of secrecy. Whenever a meeting was to be held a rose bloom was suspended from the door as a sign that no-one should enter.

There were other biblical clues to this choice of flower as an emblem of Our Lady. "Like a rose planted on the rivers I have born fruit" are the words taken from Ecclesiasticus which are spoken during the Mass of Rosary Sunday, and from the Song of Songs come the words "I am the rose of Sharon, the lily of the valleys".[9] The "Rose of the Virgin" and "Rose Mariae" are names given to the rose of Jericho, a small plant native to the sandy deserts of Arabia and there is a legend that this rose sprang from the earth beneath the feet of the Holy Family as they fled into Egypt.

As roses became associated with Our Lady, they were happily drawn into the symbolism of the enclosed garden, the inviolate womb.

In a painting by Filippino Lippi, "La Madre Pia", Our Lady is seated in a mystical garden surrounded by a balustrade beyond which there is a hedge of roses. The angels scatter rose petals over the Infant Jesus and the child St. John and four angels look on.

In another Madonna by Francia, the Mother and Child are placed in a garden enclosed by a trellis of roses, apart from all earthly connections.

In many paintings the chapelet of roses forms the enclosure, almost as if the roses themselves had taken root to grow into towering hedges. Although it is tempting and convenient to draw too many conclusions from the work of artists, the repeated choice of this subject does imply that the idea was universally popular and readily understood. As if to underline this acceptance, there is an instruction appended to the painting of "Mary, the Enclosed Garden" which tells the artist that the perimeter or enclosure need only be indicated with a garland or chapelet of roses.

Although those simple words of advice from an unknown patron to an equally unknown artist seem at first glance to be of little importance, as a clue in the search for the origin of the name of Our Lady's prayer, they are revealing, for those words imply, however casually, that the chapelet or garland of roses had joined that precious vocabulary of readily understood images.

The enclosed garden had indeed become the image to represent the enclosed womb in which was held "all heaven and earth".

Other events were to strengthen the association of Our Lady with the rose, not merely for its beauty. As the emblem "par excellence" of love, it was inevitable that the link should be further endorsed when the age of chivalry dawned in the twelfth-century.

The song of the Troubadours echoed around the courts of Europe and their theme was not merely one of chivalry but also one of love, for the crusading knight must of necessity fight not only for ideals but for love of his lady.

In an age that was Christian, when the mores of a land were inseparable from those of the Church, it was inevitable that the writers of the Church should be infected by this great wave of corteisie.

St. Bernard of Clairvaux wrote, "Mary was a rose, white for maidenhood, red for love" and he composed lengthy songs and poems to Our Lady and later St. Francis of Assisi chose for his love the Lady Poverty.

To those outside the Catholic Church, the term "our" Lady is frequently misunderstood and according to Mrs. Jameson in her "Legends of the Madonna" it was first used during the age of chivalry. Young knights on their return from distant lands took part in glittering tournaments amidst banners and golden armour, and the title was frequently heard. For these knights were blessed by the Church in vows of Faith, Honour and Courtesy and they rode forth into battle for this Lady, the Mother of God, her emblem the rose emblazoned on their helmets and banners.

A slightly less colourful and more practical account is given in "Our Lady's Dowry" by Father Bridgett, which lists a witness at the canonisation of St. Thomas of Cantalupe, Bishop of Herford in 1330 who invoked "Our Lady" or Ure Lavedi as it would have been in anglo-saxon. The Italian Commissioner enquired which lady she meant, to which she replied that of course she meant the Lady of Heaven.

In any case, the rose left forever its uncomfortable place in mythology and was chosen naturally as if this had always been its true role. Man in his stumbling journey took time to understand such heavenly connections, and the rose became the special emblem of Our Lady, reaching its height in the celestial rose of Dante in the fourteenth-century.

To Dante, no other flower was of sufficient beauty to express the radiant mystery of the Incarnation. Only the rose could symbolise the fire of Divine love brought down to earth, and to him the Blessed Virgin Mary was the "rose wherein the word Divine was made Incarnate."[10]

*   *   *   *   *   *   *

The word rosary could perhaps have remained as the title given to garlands or chapelets of roses, replete with heavenly connections, used either as coronets or to decorate altars and candles, always in honour of the Blessed Virgin. However things did not rest there. In the eleventh- and twelfth-centuries collections of prayers in honour of Our Lady were being written under such titles as "The Garden of Roses" or even simply "Rosarium", not in the cloying way of a Victorian novelist, but with monastic understanding of the similarity of the loving work of a gardener and the Christian life of prayer. Gradually the roses became prayers whose tally was kept by means of beads, and the prayers are there for the sake of the mysteries of the New Testament which make up the meditations of the rosary.

For the biblical references to gardens are not restricted to the Old Testament. The three most important events of the New Testament take place in gardens; the Agony in the Garden, the Crucifixion and the Resurrection. Fra Angelico's masterpiece, "Noli me tangere" portrays the risen Christ in an enclosed garden of rare beauty in which delicate flowers and leaves increase the notion of Paradise, underlining with gentle simplicity the implication of the Resurrection. In this picture as in many others, the Redeemer is portrayed with spade in hand, to show that His work was complete.

The message that prayer and sacrifice must precede salvation so vividly illustrated by these events was not missed by the early desert monks. These holy men were the first to understand not merely the symbolic importance of a garden but in a more practical sense they compared the toil of cultivating a garden with that of a life of prayer and through both the will of God was made known to them.

When St. Anthony the Great took to the desert in the third-century he cultivated and pruned a little garden on his mountain, not only to provide herbs for himself but also for the nourishment of his visitors after their perilous journey. On one occasion an angel appeared to him, and proceeded to plait a mat with palm leaves and then pausing to pray before resuming work with the words: "Do thus, and thou shalt be saved".[11] In this way the link between work and prayer was firmly established, and the connection between gardens and prayer was forged that led eventually to the prayer of the rosary itself.

So deeply did the early hermits understand that the loving care and labour of tending a garden was a direct parallel to prayer that another desert monk, St. Phocan, remains to this day the patron saint of gardeners.

St. Phocan dwelt outside the gate of Sinope and lived, his life states quite simply, by cultivating a garden. Under Diocletian orders were sent out for his arrest and soldiers were despatched to find him. Having lost their way, the men stopped at the home of the saint, who moved by pity, took them in and cared lovingly for them. Under the warmth of his kindness, they explained their task whereupon the saint promised to reward their search the following day. After his guests had retired to bed, St. Phocan went into the garden and in prayer he prepared his grave. In the morning he led the soldiers into the garden explaining his identity and there amongst his flowers he died.

From these early beginnings the importance of gardening in Christian monasticism was firmly established, and further endorsed by St. Benedict in his Rule which laid down strict instruction on the form and cultivation of the monastery garden. There is in existence a plan of the ideal Benedictine monastery which was drawn up for the Abbot of St. Gall in Switzerland in the middle of the ninth-century. The plan shows three gardens, one of medicinal herbs which are listed in great detail, the kitchen garden with eighteen beds containing onions, garlic, leeks and shallots and thirdly, the orchard with fruit trees planted in straight lines so that the graves of the monks could be laid between them.[12] In later centuries roses were planted in the monk's cemetery in anticipation of Paradise and of Our Lady who awaited them in heaven.[13] St. Benedict himself cultivated flowers, but lest he should succumb to the worldly joy of his little garden, he also grew brambles to mortify his flesh. There is a legend that describes a visit by St. Francis to Subiaco in 1216 in which these brambles were miraculously transformed into roses, and the garden is preserved to this day.

Cardinal Newman has described the Benedictines as the custodians of civilisation throughout the dark ages, for while danger and chaos held sway elsewhere, within the monastery walls the monks continued their life of prayer and work as instructed by the Rule, laid down in the sixth-century. They became a lifeline to the community not only in the spiritual sense, but also for their teaching and farming expertise. Benedictine land was farmed for grain and the traditional water fountain of the early Paradise gardens was translated into large fish ponds seething with carp for the refectory table. Amongst the fruit orchards beyond the vineyards, beehives stood in serried ranks and herb gardens proliferated.

In 840, Walafrid Strabo, a Benedictine monk, wrote a poem entitled the "Little Garden" which relates in some detail the plants that were grown at the time of Charlemagne. Although written over a thousand years ago, it presents a vivid picture of the old monk toiling over his garden as he struggled with the nettles, whose roots were like "basket-work". The discouragement is only fleeting for he quickly passes on to praise the beauty of his favourite plants, dwelling on the beauties of the lily and the rose, considered by some to be the emblems of the martyrs.

The Cistercians, however, lived in cells constructed in such a manner that no view of other humans was possible and each cell led into a private garden in which the inhabitant grew herbs to sustain his frugal existence.

In the solid uncompromising stone remains of Mount Grace Priory in Yorkshire, where no concession was made to beauty, the silent ruins bear witness to a life of stark simplicity where no diversion could be allowed and the gardens, once loved and laboured over, lie abandoned to a riot of weeds. And yet occasionaly the eye is caught by wild flowers happily growing amidst the chaos, to proclaim that all is never lost.

To those intrepid monks, their gardens were not seen as a diversion but as an echo of Paradise to which all must aspire. Even so not everyone was capable of such perfection, and there must have been occasions when the love of gardening and pride in his own industry tempted the lonely monk to peer over the wall at his neighbour's work, or even to succumb to a moment of earthly pride in the results of his labours. Some indeed became so enthralled by their gardens that a writer named Heffad of Lands-perg in a work entitled *Hortus Deliciarum*, related the sad fate of a monk who had climbed to the top of the ladder of holiness only to glance down at his beloved garden, thereby losing his balance and falling to the ground, forfeiting all for the love of his earthly paradise.

In less enclosed orders, paradise gardens were created and placed symbolically near the entrance to the abbey church. This was in part an influence of the early eastern gardens, for glowing accounts of Persian gardens were sent home by the Ambassadors to the courts of the Caliphs of Baghdad, tales of luxurious lawns usually divided by paths with a central fountain, inhabited by peacocks and exotic birds. These gardens were aptly named paradise gardens.

Bishop Etholwold (908-984) of Winchester built an abbey at Thorne later described by William of Malmesbury as being set in a paradise. The paradise garden in this case was the domain of the sacristan, for here he grew flowers, mainly roses and lilies, for the decoration of the Church.

In addition to the altars, all the shrines and statues of the saints and even the candles were encircled with flowers, for the garland or circle was not only decorative but a constant reminder of the "enclosed garden", forshadowing the circle of beads which would gather men's thoughts to the mystery of the Incarnation.

Sometimes the symbolism was not restricted to the flower of the rose alone but the whole bush or tree was used to illustrate the undoubted labour required to achieve sanctity.

In an engraving of the sixteenth-century, three Dominican monks, Joseph Sprenger, Alanus du Rupe and St. Dominic himself, are to be seen tending a rose tree within an enclosed garden above which Our Lady extends in her hand a circle of rosary beads.

The theme of the rose tree is used again with great beauty in the *Secret of the Rosary* written in the seventeenth-century by St. Louis de Montfort. The book opens with the author's dedication offered in the form of roses, thus a white rose for priests, a red rose for sinners and a mystical rose tree for devout souls. This last dedication he elaborates thus: "Its green leaves are the joyful mysteries, the thorns the sorrowful ones, and the flowers the glorious mysteries . . . eventually this little seed will grow so great that the birds of heaven will dwell in it and make their nests there. Its shade will shelter them from the scorching heat of the sun and its· great height will keep them safe from the wild beasts on the ground." He concludes the dedications with a rosebud for children. The body of the book is divided into fifty small sections reflecting the number of Aves in the Psalter, each one entitled numerically as a rose, and it remains the most loved work on the subject of the rosary.

This preoccupation with plants and prayer was not in the least sentimental. In most cases the monks existed on the produce they eked from the soil and the rigours of their lives left little room for day dreaming, nor did they show any inclination to do so.

It was rather a recognition of the humble role of the gardener, of the fleeting glimpse of mortality enshrined in the earth to which all must return, and above all the lesson to be learnt from the quiet attendance on the will of God.

St. Louis de Montfort, more than any writer before or after his own time, was drawing the threads together, for in his writing he illustrates in a direct way the feelings of those early desert hermits with their more primitive but no less inspiring awareness of the Garden of Paradise in their life of prayer. As writers described this timeless connection, so the painters by their masterpieces achieved the same message. But while the experts held sway, the prayer of the rosary had quietly slipped into the hands of the faithful, for the secret of the rosary lay not so much in the spoken as in the unspoken word. All these thoughts were well understood

and expressed with sweet simplicity by an anonymous writer of
the thirteenth-century:

> "Lady, flower of alle thing
> Rosa sine spina
> Thou bere Jesu, heven king
> Gratia divina."

CHAPTER TWO

Ring a ring of roses
A pocket full of posies
Atishoo atishoo
We all fall down.

Anon.

CAXTON'S PRINT OF CHAUCER — *From an Illuminated Manu-script at the British Library.*

CHAPTER TWO

ALTHOUGH the beads of the rosary we hold in our hands today seem so uncomplicated, it is surprising to find how long the various features took to become recognisable. More than any one influence, it was the spiritual experience of pious souls spread over a considerable passage of time, that eventually helped to form the rosary as we know it.

Prayer must be the beginning and the first element of the rosary. The root from which the second and third elements grow is formed by the Paternosters and Aves recited in honour of the joys, sorrows and glories from the life of Our Lord from the New Testament.

Under the influence of the many pilgrimages undertaken during the Middle Ages, it was natural that movement and rhythm should become an important part of the rosary, and finally it is above all a prayer of meditation, the vital ingredient that came last of all.

The choice of prayers was undoubtedly influenced by the religious traditions of England where devotion to Mary was well established during the Middle Ages. Named Albion, after the scented white rosa-alba, England was the acknowledged dower of Our Lady.

Until recently there was a picture in the English College in Rome which confirms the view that although no precise date is known for the official naming of Our Lady's dower, the idea was familiar enough in the fourteenth-century.

The picture shows King Richard II and his Queen assisted by St. John the Baptist humbly offering England to Our Lady while she smiles her acceptance. Despite the upheavals of later centuries, that title has never been formally relinquished and to this day England remains Our Lady's dowry.

There are few traces left today, although probably more than can at first be recognised. Some places still bear lingering witness, such as Ottery St. Mary or St. Mary Clyst in Devon, St. Mary Bourne in Hampshire, in London the familiar Marylebone which comes from Mary la Bonne, and there are others too numerous to mention.

But these are merely ghostly signposts to a land where once the chapels and shrines throughout the countryside were a constant reminder of the love borne by the people for Mary, a place in which St. George could be described by his biographer as "Our Lady's Knight" for he was and is the patron of her dowry.

It is idle curiosity to wonder how many of those who proudly wear the rose of England on their sports shirts have any knowledge of its origin for little is known today of the importance given to the Blessed Virgin in England before the Reformation, and of how deeply that affection was woven into the culture of the time.

In pre-Reformation days, England had sixteen hundred churches to proclaim devotion to Our Lady, not to mention the religious houses, colleges and shrines under her patronage.

This picture does seem to disprove the idea that true recognition of Mary is some strange continental habit. There is ample evidence that the reverse is true and we have no need to borrow such terms as the "Madonna" from the Italians, for in England the title of the "Blissful Maiden" or Chaucer's "Blissful Quene" date from a far earlier time.

The emphasis placed on Marian devotion is frequently misinterpreted and there is a clear distinction to be drawn. It is in effect devotion through Mary, for as the Mother of God, her life was spent in honouring her Son and Catholic teaching has always maintained that man should honour the Blessed Virgin by following her example.

In this country, the custom of venerating Our Lady stretches back to the fifth-century at least. William of Malmesbury described the Oratory of Glastonbury, built in 430 A.D. as "a holy and ancient spot, chosen and sanctified by God, in honour of the Immaculate Virgin Mary, Mother of God".[1]

From the time of St. Augustine, churches have been built in her honour in England, and poems and prayers composed in praise of the role of the Blessed Virgin as mediatrix with her Son. The learned Cistercian Abbot, Aelred of Rievaulx whose writings followed the tradition laid down by earlier monks, expressed this complex teaching to his followers thus: "The greatness of Mary's love for men is proved by the many miracles and many visions by which the Lord deigns to show that she especially intercedes with her Son for the whole human race. It is vain for me to even attempt to show how great is her charity; no human mind is able to conceive it."[2]

Throughout the Dark Ages, from the fall of the Roman Empire until the millennium, the turbulent nature of the time meant that for most people life was full of suffering. Hardship and disaster were their constant companions as plagues and wars overtook them with little or no warning and through all these calamities it seemed as though Mary, their unearthly mother, would be their refuge and strength in an age of great paternalism and cruelty.

The Venerable Bede alone seems to shine like a beacon in the wilderness of those times, writing from the draughty abbey of Whitby in the eighth-century and his many texts and sermons bear witness to his devotion for Our Lady.

At first he seemed intent on proving the holiness of the Blessed Virgin, but having proved that beyond doubt, he turned to dwell upon her joys. This link with the mysteries of the rosary and also the convenience of his name have frequently earned for him the authorship of the rosary, and although this was not so, the theory would undoubtedly have appealed to that holy man.

The Venerable Bede died in 735, and in the year of his death another great Benedictine named Alcuin was born, who was to spend many years of his life in York before going for a time to the courts of Charlemagne. He, too, was a great devotee of Mary and on one occasion he sent home a description of his cell in Tours which he had decorated with white lilies and red roses in her honour.

Before he travelled to France in 780, whilst Charlemagne was setting out to do battle with the Saracens and the cries of Roland were echoing around the valley of Roncevalles, Alcuin composed his mass in honor of Our Lady, known to all as the Mary Mass. Although as St. Augustine pointed out, Mass can be offered to God alone, the Mary Mass is one in which the Blessed Virgin is commemorated.

The Mary Mass became very popular and there were numerous occasions when bequests were made to maintain the St. Mary priest as he was called, and in many houses the Mary Mass was celebrated every day in a private chapel. As dawn broke the bell known as the Mary bell rang to awaken everyone and announce the hour of prayer.

In the time of King Alfred laws had been passed to ensure that all his subjects were able to join in the festivities of feast days. The Assumption on August 15th was known as "St. Mary Mass in Harvest" and the new laws gave freemen a week's holiday before the feast. In Walsingham, King Henry III granted the right to hold a fair lasting six days before Our Lady's birthday in September.

Not everyone responded with exemplary piety and some bishops complained loudly about the markets and fairs which were held on these special days. The early Mass on Our Lady's feast day was known to many as the glutton Mass for those who were up in time to attend were then free for the rest of the day.

In the Valor Ecclesiasticus there is mention of a sum of money paid to the clerics and choristers who sang daily the Mass of the Blessed Virgin in Salisbury Cathedral, and in 1215 land was given by the Bishop of St. Paul's in London to the poor clerks of the choir who sang the office of Our Lady after the Mary Mass.

Some feasts had been celebrated for hundreds of years, indeed when St. Augustine led his followers to Canterbury in the sixth-century he found that the feast of the Purification had become part of the calendar under the influence of Roman missionaries of earlier times.[3]

The feast of the Immaculate Conception was of particular importance in England for it was first celebrated in this country, an enterprise which caused heated controversy between the English and French clergy. The feast was instituted by St. Anselm who came to England from the Abbey of Bec in the time of William Rufus.

When the Dark Ages drew to a close in the eleventh-century, the devotion to Mary that had steadily grown over the preceding centuries emerged on a wave of enthusiasm. In this period of peace and relative prosperity, then as throughout history, gardening become a popular pastime. Under the Normans, English gardens became areas of great beauty and as many of the Norman lords had returned to this land from conquering Southern Italy and Moorish Spain, the influence of the eastern Garden of Paradise became apparent. Perhaps some of the gardeners themselves were Norman soldiers. To stroll amongst these scented flowers and lawns must have induced an air of thoughtful contemplation wholly unknown until then and not surprisingly Mary is acknowledged in the naming of the flowers. The snowdrop was known as "Our Lady of February", lungwort as "Our Lady's milk-worte" from the Annunciation; marigolds belonged to all her feasts, and it was well known that the lily bloomed from the Visitation to St. Swithuns.

These days of festivity naturally led people to associate joy with the name of Mary, and it is here that the teaching of the Venerable Bede undoubtedly influenced the foundation of the rosary.

Much of the popularity of the joys is said also to have been due to St. Thomas à Becket, who was the Archbishop of Canterbury during the turbulent reign of King Henry II. St. Thomas was a hero to his followers for he defended the rights of the Church with a fervour that was to cost him his life. In quieter moments he composed a hymn on the seven joys of Our Lady, listing the visiting of the Magi, the Finding in the Temple, the Annunciation, the Birth of Christ, the Resurrection, the Ascension and the

Assumption. The first two joys were frequently omitted to leave five although the number did vary, for John of Gaunt left fifteen pieces of silver to the Carmelites in London in honour of fifteen joys.

As if to find some practical way of demonstrating this new interest in the joys of Mary, the custom grew of lighting candles before her statue. Usually five in number to reflect the five wounds of Christ, these candles were frequently decorated with garlands of flowers and known as "gauds", and later the word was used to describe the large bead that separates the Ave beads from the Paternoster, between the mysteries.

The most elaborate arrangements were made to ensure that after the death of the supplicant the candle would continue to burn before Our Lady's statue, and even cattle or sheep were left to support the cost. The custom was not restricted to country people for King Henry VIII kept candles burning at the shrines of Our Lady of Doncaster and Walsingham known as King's candles.

A detailed instruction on the recitation of prayers with the five joys of Our Lady is to be found in the *Ancren Riwle*, the rule set down by the Bishop of Salisbury for the nuns of a convent at Tarrent in Dorset. Writing early in the thirteenth-century, the Bishop sets out prayers on the joys of Mary, each consisting of a short dissertation commencing with the words "Sweet Lady, St. Mary" and treating in turn the Annunciation, the Birth, the Resurrection, the Ascension and the Coronation of Our Lady in Heaven. After each reading, five Hail Mary's are to be recited and he adds "After her five highest joys count in the anthems. Cause to be written on a scroll what ye do not know by heart".

The Bishop of Salisbury can have little suspected that his gentle rule for those Dorsetshire nuns would continue to be a source of inspiration for hundreds of years to come. Written with a mixture of humility and severity, it is full of practical means of achieving sanctity and as is only natural in the rugged country existence of the place and time, he often illustrates his point with down-to-earth simplicity.

On the subject of talkativeness, he is firm: "Eve in Paradise held a long conversation with the serpent, and told him all the lessons that God had taught her and Adam concerning the apple; thus the fiend by her talk understood, at once, her weakness, and found out the way to ruin her. Our Lady, Saint Mary, acted in quite a different manner. She told the Angel no tale, but asked him briefly that which she wanted to know. Do you, my dear sister, imitate Our Lady and not the cackling Eve. Wherefore, let an anchoress, whatsoever she be, keep silence as much as ever can and may. Let her not have the hen's nature; when the hen has laid she must needs to cackle. And what does she get by it? Straightway comes the chough and robs her of her eggs and devours all that of which she should have brought forth the live birds. And just so the wicked chough, the devil . . . "

On the subject of the joys of Mary he instructed them to pray "Sweet Lady, Saint Mary, receive my salutation with the same "Ave" and make me to think little of every outward delight, and comfort me within, and by thy merits procure for me the joy of heaven." He concludes his rule with the words "As often as ye read anything in this book greet the Lady with an Ave Maria and for him who made this rule, and for him who wrote it and took pains about it. Moderate enough I am, who asks so little", and one can only imagine that they must have been happy to do as he wished.[4]

The joys that are honoured today are the Annunciation, the Visitation of Our Lady to her cousin Elizabeth, the Birth of Our Lord, the Presentation in the Temple, and the Finding of the Child Jesus in the Temple. Having established this interest in the joys of Our Lady, thoughts turned instinctively to the next subject of the rosary, for the realisation that sorrow must accompany joy was born constant testimony in their own harsh existence. They were deeply aware of the figure weeping at the foot of the Cross and the example of holiness through suffering became in turn the subject of wrapt attention.

The title "Our Lady of Pity" was in frequent use in England,

meaning Our Lady of Suffering. Many churches had statues por-
traying Mary grieving over the body of her Son as He was taken
from the Cross, and these were known as pietas.

In the thirteenth-century, St. Edmund wrote: "You ought also
to meditate on the most sweet Virgin Mary, with what anguish
she was filled when she stood at the right hand side of her most
sweet Son."[5]

Suffering was no stranger in their lives and her example
brought a vision and inspiration mingled with consolation so
deep as to be almost beyond human understanding. The sorrows
were referred to as the "Dolors of Our Lady" and on Good Friday
and Holy Saturday, plays were enacted in many villages with
vivid portrayals of such subjects as Mary Magdalen's mourning
and lamenting to St. Joseph, and the scene at the sepulchre.

The great writers of the Church, abbots such as Oelfric, Anselm
and Aelric wrote at length on such subjects as Simeon's prophecy,
and various forms of prayer concentrating on this aspect of the life
of the Blessed Virgin are to be found in a small prayer book entitled "Of the Compassion of Our Lady" which instructs the laity
in a form of devotion that was easier to learn and recite than the
full office, consisting of a short lesson on the events in the passion
and death of Our Lord, each one preceded by five Paternosters
and five Aves. Each reading together with the prayers was to be
said at different hours of the day thus enabling the laity to pray
the "hours" as was the custom in the great religious houses.

The advantage of praying these particular mysteries in the form
of the "hours" lay in the sense of timing each subject with the actual hour of its happening in the day of Our Lord's passion, and
they were written in verse and therefore easy to remember,
finishing with the verse "Compline is the end of the day; and at
the end of our life we have most need of Our Lady's help."[6] The
Sorrowful Mysteries today differ slightly and are the Agony of
Our Lord in the Garden of Gethsemane, the Scourging at the
Pillar, the Crowning with Thorns, the Carrying of the Cross and
the Death on the Cross.

The Glorious Mysteries were then turned to and again the writings are prolific on such subjects as the Assumption and the Coronation in Heaven of Mary. Today we celebrate the Resurrection, the Ascension, the Descent of the Holy Spirit on the Apostles, the Assumption of Our Lady and finally the Coronation in Heaven of Our Lady.

While the three "humours" of the rosary were emerging, the choice of prayers to accompany these mysteries was also being made.

Psalms were adapted in praise of Mary, especially in England and for those unable to read or remember the psalms, expression was given to their thoughts by repeating the greeting of the Angel Gabriel at the Annunciation. Both the Venerable Bede and St. Aelred, Abbot of Rievaulx wrote long sermons on the subject of the Annunciation, and the Angelic Salutation formed part of their prayer.

By the end of the twelfth-century the clergy of Paris were listing the Ave Maria together with the Credo and Paternoster as prayers that the faithful were required to know.

In England the same instructions were given by St. Richard of Chichester in 1246 and the Bishop of Durham followed suit in 1255. Although the Ave Maria consisted of the Angelic Salutation alone, the fact that it was confidently referred to by the first two words, as was the Paternoster, infers that it was already very familiar to all. The words of St. Elizabeth, "Blessed is the fruit of thy womb" were added shortly after this date, and thus it remained until St. Bernardino of Sienna added the last words in the middle of the fifteenth-century.

In the *Reliquae Antiquae* there are many examples of the various forms of the Ave Maria, and there is one which is said to date from a manuscript of the thirteenth-century:

> Marie ful off grace, weel de be,
> Godd of hevene be with thee,
> Oure alle wimmen bliscedd tu be,
> So be the bern datt is boren of thee.[7]

The total recited usually seems to have been one hundred and fifty, reflecting the number of psalms in the Psalter of St. David on which every monastery of the time based the daily worship. The tally reached almost mythological heights, especially in Ireland, where the influence of St. Patrick had further divided the number into three, known as the "three fifties". Even in the legend of King Arthur and his Knights of the Round Table, an allegory for man's search for Paradise, the number of his knights was carefully chosen to reflect the number of psalms in the Psalter.

In the eleventh-century, the first acknowledged step towards the arrangement of the rosary was taken by St. Anselm, then Archbishop of Canterbury. He composed a prayer to Mary which was based on the psalms and consisted of one hundred and fifty verses, which he divided into three, each verse commencing with the word "ave".

The prayer, which was written for his monks at Canterbury to recite each day, must have been offered many times for the saint himself as he struggled with the King over the respective rights of the Church and Crown. He named this prayer "Our Lady's Psalter", the first official prayer of this name, and the legends that sprung up at the time give some idea of the interest that greeted St. Anselm's Psalter.

One, entitled "How Our Levidi's Sauter was first Founde" comes from a Scottish manuscript which relates the story of a young man saying his fifty Aves daily. Our Lady appeared before him meanly dressed and when he enquired the reason for this, she replied that this was due to the short measure of his prayer, and more were needed.[8]

But it was not only the legends that bore witness to the affection in which Mary was held. There is a wall painting in a church which is no longer Catholic, but dating from early Catholic days, which illustrates this trust in Our Lady the Advocate.

The somewhat primitive picture relates the story of St. Michael, weighing the souls of the dead. There he stands, the judge of souls with the scales of justice in one hand and in the other a flaming sword, apparently unaware and unperturbed by whatever the result might be.

In one panier is a little soul, just dead, who peers anxiously at the other panier, which is weighed down by a large bundle marked "sins". To his horror, the scale is drawn further down by a crowd of little devils. What he cannot see is the figure of the Mother of God, standing behind him. She observes all that is happening, has realised that two can play at that game, and she is dropping her rosary, bead by bead, into the scale of the poor frightened soul, so that to his amazement his scale is more heavily weighed down.[9]

In the fourteenth-century, a famous Carthusian monk, Henry Egher, claimed to have had a remarkable vision of Our Lady in which she taught him how to say the "Psalter" in her honour. This he described to one of the priors of his order in England, and within a very short space of time, the prayer became known throughout the country, with far reaching effects.

Eton College was founded in honor of Our Lady by Henry II, and the original seal of the college depicts the Assumption of the Virgin with the Royal Arms inscribed beneath. The statutes of the College required the students to say each day "the complete psalter of the Blessed Virgin consisting of a Credo, fifteen Paters and one hundred and fifty Ave Marias", and this was in accordance with the instructions of Our Lady to the Carthusian monk. The choristers were instructed to recite the hours of Mary each day, and a final practical note required that each scholar should recite the Office of Our Lady whilst making his bed. Other institutions, including King's College, Cambridge, received similar instructions and the choristers were obliged to recite the hours of Mary each day.

These prayers differed only slightly from "Our Lady's Psalter" composed by St. Anselm and had been familiar to people in England since the eleventh-century, long before the prayer of the rosary was officially acknowledged and certainly before the Dominican influence emerged.

Much of the liturgy of the Church was intended to be sung, and the ave-psalm-psalter, as it became known, was no exception. Indeed the word "psalter" literally means a musical instrument of ten strings. Sometimes chanted within the lofty transepts of abbeys, on other occasions the psalter was sung in the open air by pilgrims on their way to any of the multitude of shrines dedicated to their most gracious Advocate. The universal popularity of pilgrimages in the Middle Ages had a profound influence on the element of rhythm and movement in the prayer of the rosary, and from the beginning Christians have acknowledged that there is a spiritual advantage in reciting the prayer in procession.

In those days, pilgrimages were a way of life and the constant traveling to and fro across Europe to all the shrines of Christendom was never ceasing. The pilgrim was treated with great respect and honour, so much so that on one occasion during the wars against France in the fourteenth-century an Englishman was taken prisoner in Cahors but released immediately when it was realised that he was on his way to the shrine of Our Lady of Rocamadour.

The shrine of Our Lady of Walsingham was one of the most popular of the great centres of pilgrimage in the Middle Ages, and according to the historian Harrod, "almost from the foundation of the priory to the dissolution there was one unceasing movement of pilgrims to and from Walsingham."

Some of the shrines dedicated to Mary are of great antiquity, such a the chapel at Glastonbury which was reputedly founded when St. Joseph of Arimathea came to England in AD 63 and legend has it that the wattles for the first chapel of Our Lady were made from his staff which took root when he thrust it into the ground. William of Malmesbury lists the many kings and others who sought to be buried there to await judgement under the protection of Our Lady. At the shrine of Our Lady of Storrington blessed by Pope Leo XIII, the Blessed Virgin was venerated as Our Lady of England, the only place using that title.

There were numerous shrines of less fame whose origins are

often obscured by legend. There is frequently some difficulty in discovering precisely why a certain place was chosen, but it was usually in thanksgiving for blessings received or because a miracle was reported to have occurred in a certain place.

The people of the Middle Ages lived in an age that was not sceptical and they fully expected these things to happen, for most of these stories were prompted by a deep religious fervour that gave great gaiety of heart on one hand, and on the other a profound sense of humility.

For the most part we have to rely on the chroniclers who usually saved their ink for the famous. In 1240 King Henry III sent an oak from the forest of Windsor to provide wood for the roof of the Chapel of Our Lady of Caversham where the Benedictines had built a bridge across the Thames from the Abbey at Reading. This place of pilgrimage became very popular and from the letters of Henry VIII we learn that in September 1517 "offering by the King at Our Lady of Caversham 18s.4d."[10] and another offering was made in 1520. In another volume of these letters Sir Robert Wingfield, writing to Wolsey in 1532 recounts "this morning the King rode forth right early to hunt and the Queen is ridden to Our Lady of Caversham." It was to be the last pilgrimage of Katherine of Aragon as recognised Queen of England.

In Wales the shrine of Our Lady of Pen-Rhys was much revered particularly for its association with the rosary. Founded in 1179 it was built in rolling hills 1,000 feet above the Rhondda Valley, surrounded by the blue mountains. Llwellyn ap Hywell, a Welsh poet of the fifteenth-century wrote "a goodly place it is, with its summit and wooded slope, and the Virgin sanctuary beside the high forest. There is enthroned her image; there is pardeon to be gained in the five joys of Mary." It was demolished by Cromwell in 1538.

A glimpse at the every day working of these shrines is revealed by the list of bequests made by pilgrims and benefactors. Of the many gifts laid at the foot of the altar, perhaps the most perplexing is the number of girdles. But further search reveals that it was the custom for a woman expecting the birth of a child to wear a belt inscribed with the Magnificat in honour of Our Lady and in the hope of a safe delivery.

One of the many examples of this is provided by Constance Bigod who left her girdle worked with silver and gilt to Our Lady of Doncaster in 1449. In 1382 the Earl of Suffolk left a silver statuette of a fully armed man on a horse perhaps to remind Our Lady that he was off to fight the French. Both instances demonstrate a marvellously practical approach and show how intimately this trust in Mary was woven into their lives.

At Doncaster the Carmelite friars founded their house in 1350 with the help of John of Gaunt, and through the years many pilgrims wound their way across the deep and treacherous river to this shrine. Henry VII visited Our Lady of Doncaster on his way north after his coronation as did his daughter Margaret on her progress to Scotland to marry James IV and so the royal peregrinations continued.

There was one Yorkshireman, however, whose visit was indeed noted and remembered with pride and sadness. For it was at the shrine of Our Lady of Doncaster that Robert Aske gathered the chivalry of Northern England on an October day in 1536. Beneath a banner showing the five wounds of Christ, some 30,000 men met the royal army King Henry VIII had sent to meet them. Those who made up this gathering were veteran soldiers, peaceful countrymen and boys who had been brought up to look with awe on the monasteries so richly supported by the piety of their ancestors, and made holy by the traditions of four centuries, the place where their fathers were buried and the schools where they themselves were taught.

To the abbots and monks they turned as to trusted and wise friends. The pillars of their society were being wrenched from them and Robert Aske was leading them not against the King, but against his enemies and theirs. The King's anger erupted and this brave lawyer who had emerged from obscurity went to the gallows with many of his followers. But they were not forgotten and today the statue of Our Lady of Doncaster is in the Lady Chapel of the Church of St. Peter and St. Paul in that town.

Perhaps the most telling of all memories of this great centre of mediaeval pilgrimage, when other events have faded into history, is the simple bequest of one Alice West: "To Our Lady of Doncaster; my best bedes."

Many of the shrines were dismantled during the time of the Reformation and the accounts make sorry reading, for the custom of processing and worshipping at these holy places had become part of the English way of life and their destruction was a blow from which it took centuries to recover. There were countless stories of the attempts made to preserve the remains and in one place there is a bleak description of a procession of pilgrims encircling the charred remains of their shrine in the moonlight, while reciting the rosary in the night air.

Even today the strange circles seen sometimes etched on hillsides, too old for memories to recall, may well be the remains of early shrines. As processions reached their destination, the pilgrims fell to their knees and encircled the shrine in penance and this custom was repeated within the precincts of large abbeys and cathedrals, forming well-worn circles over years of kneeling prayer.

The circle is so much a part of our lives that we take for granted the influence that it has on almost all that surrounds us. Children with unerring instinct seek to join hands and form a circle of dance and some people think that "ring a ring of roses" comes from "ring a rosary" with the "atishoo atishoo" symbolising the Holy Spirit at the Annunciation and at Pentecost. In Germany they sing "ringel, ringel, rosen crantz", ring a ring a rosary".

The rhythm of the prayer of the rosary is reduced nowadays to the steady movement of hands on beads and the repetition of prayer, but in the early centuries prayer was held to be a physical as well as a mental exercise. The early Syrian hermits repeatedly threw themselves to the ground during their prayer and their swollen knees and torn hands were the subject of much comment and admiration.

The Irish monks of St. Patrick prayed with their arms out-stretched in the form of a cross, known as the "crossfigil" and the original recitation of Our Lady's Psalter entailed fifty Aves, each one accompanied by a genuflection. King, later Saint, Louis of France "knelt down every day fifty times, and in the evening and each time he stood upright, and then knelt down anew, and each time he then knelt down he said very slowly an "Ave Maria".[11]

Although no doubt the main reason for these movements was the desire to make a total offering to God of mind and body, there must have been an element of keeping the mind alert as a sentry on duty marches back and forth to keep his wits about him.

In the Middle Ages there was a great sense of movement in prayer, in a joyous and practical sense, and this is shown vividly in a popular legend of the time known as "Our Lady's Tumbler".

The tale describes the search of a renowned acrobat for a life of holiness and prayer within the Abbey of Clairvaux, and of his increasing sense of failure at his inability to pray with the same air of peace and serenity as those around him. Finding himself alone in the abbey church one day, he abandoned himself to joyful acrobatics. Peering around a pillar, his astonished fellow monks saw Our Lady, surrounded by angels, descending from the altar to approach their new brother with great joy. To the end of his day, the story relates, Our Lady's Tumbler danced his prayer and was much loved by his fellow monks.

This sense of rhythm is a vital part of the rosary for the repetition of prayer creates a melodic background to the last and most important element of the prayer.

* * * * * * *

The ave-psalm-psalter remained the form and style of Our Lady's prayer until the early fourteenth-century and usually, especially in England, the Aves were repeated in honour of the joys and hence their frequent name the "gaudyes". Increasingly the number of one hundred and fifty was divided into three fifties.

The third element of the rosary, was the one which took the longest to develop, and it was not until the fifteenth-century that meditation, rather than prayer in honour of a subject, became an accepted part of the rosary. In the legend of "How Our Levidi's Sauter was first Founde", Our Lady instructed her client to recite the first fifty in the morning in honour of the Annunciation, the second at noon in honour of the Nativity, and the third in the evening in honour of her Assumption and Glory in Heaven. At this stage there was no direct suggestion of meditation, rather the offering in honour of some specific subject.

Gradually the prayer developed into one of meditation, for Our Lady was named "Our Lady of Wisdom" and in the rosary, the story of Our Lord's life is arranged by His mother for us to dwell upon following the example she gave, for "His Mother Mary kept all these words, pondering them in her heart."[12]

The word contemplation comes from the Persian word *templum*, which was used to describe enclosures within their gardens, areas set aside for peaceful reflection, enclosed by immense hedges to enhance the impression of other-worldness, and it is apt that Our Lady's prayer of the rosary, the rose garden, should be one of devout recollection.

The length of time spent in prayer and meditation by monks and nuns of the early Church would be almost impossible to exaggerate, for every waking hour was spent in contemplation and worship of God. For people of the twentieth-century whose constant cry is "there is no time" it is a sobering thought to realise that these people quite literally gave their lives to God, for they considered that as man is made in the image of God, it is natural and right that the soul should turn at all times to its Creator. Not in the morbid way of the nuns of Tarrent who were so enclosed that even their windows had to be the smallest and most narrow, covered in black cloth, but in the joyful way of St. Francis of Assisi and St. Clare. To them the birds, flowers, trees and sunlight were not luxuries but the word of God, as they were two centuries later to Fra Angelico whose meditative prayer is there for all to see glowing from the walls of his Dominican monastery of San Marco in Florence. Fra Angelico wished to inspire the Christian beholder with a longing for the Garden of Eden and he portrayed many of the subjects of the mysteries of the rosary.

As we gaze into his vision of the events of the life of Christ painted in great simplicity and purity of colour on the walls of the cells of his fellow monks, it is not difficult to imagine the incredulity of his brothers in the monastery as he moved from cell to cell. In each he painted a fresco which should be seem as a visual prayer and perhaps that is why they appear to be timeless. In fact only as an afterthought does the onlooker realise how immediately Fra Angelico viewed his subject; thus Mary is seated peacefully on a monk's stool beneath the graceful arches of the cloister of San Marco when the angel Gabriel visits her. Far from displaying any sign of the dramatic news the angel has for Our Lady, his expression is one of devotion and peace, and the only indication given of his importance is in the brilliant rainbow of his wings and even they are blended into the leafy shadows.

In the same way he often includes a brother monk with the saints in the scenes he depicts, as for example in the dramatic picture of the Holy Sepulchre. We see Mary and the holy women gazing into the empty tomb in statuesque amazement and there behind the angel a monk smiles with such affection that we can only smile with him. In this sense of immediacy there was no lack of imagination but an awareness of the timeless quality of the events in the life of Christ that enabled Fra Angelico to see them all around him, in the peaceful cloisters in the heart of Florence with a intimacy of prayer that was so much part of his own life of meditation, reminiscent of the legend of Our Lady's Tumbler.

The problem is not therefore one of discovering the time when meditation began to be part of the life of prayer but rather one of deciding when outside events so invaded the peace of the monastery that something had to be done to ensure that no greater encroachment could be made.

Probably that time came when the monks began to take on their work of illumination and writing, and still more when they went out into the world to teach.

The laity also needed some guidelines to help them for although the Angelus bell continued to ring in every village in England until the time of the Reformation, there must have been many distractions just as there are today.

In the fourteenth-century a Carthusian monk, known as Dominic of Prussia, composed fifty *clausulae* or phrases to be added to the Aves, each one introducing a meditation of the life of Our Lord, and they follow the pattern of the meditations we have to this day. For example, for the Annunciation, he wrote: "Hail Mary, full of grace, blessed is the fruit of thy womb Jesus Christ, Whom at the angel's word thou didst conceive of the Holy Ghost Amen."[13]

From this came the expression "Reading the Rosary" and it prompted the printing of many books on this method of reciting the rosary, and these were usually illustrated with pictures to encourage meditation.

In 1328 a Dominican of Soissons composed three books each of which contained fifty legends or gaudia in honour of the Blessed Virgin, with instructions to "remember" events in Our Lord's life, and rather mysteriously he wrote in the margin the words ROS or ROSARI rather than mention his own name. Another Dominican, Romeus de Livia, was reported to have held in his hands a knotted string on which to count his Aves, while he thought "upon Child Jesus and His mother Mary."

From this time the popularity of the rosary spread throughout Europe and different orders claimed varying arrangements of the prayer for their own. For example the rosary of Our Lady of Consolation belongs to the Augustinian order, and consists of twelve Paternosters and twelve Aves in honour of the twelve Apostles.

The Franciscan crown as it is known, consists of seven Paternosters and ten Aves in honour of seven joys, and in the sixteenth-century the Corona of Our Lady (frequently confused with the garland or chapelet of the rosary, but in fact quite separate) which consisted of sixty-three Aves and seven Paternosters, to correspond with the sixty-three years of Our Lady's life.

The Corona was made up of six decades with the three extra beads making up the pendant attached to the circle of beads, and this is thought to be the reason for those extra beads which rosaries carry today. Others think that these three are to be prayed for faith, hope and charity to enable the rosary to be offered more devoutly.

The rosary in general use today is the Dominican rosary which is made up of one hundred and fifty Aves, fifteen Paternosters and fifteen Glorias divided into three fifties. The wishes of those early English Christians expressed so clearly in the legend of "Our Levedi's Sauter" have been faithfully followed and the Joyful Mysteries are followed by the Sorrowful, and then the Glorious Mysteries of the life of Christ.

The element of rhythm, so vital a part of the rosary, is followed in the sequence of different mysteries which fall on different days of the week, and as the days run into months, the months to years, so the continual cycle of prayer is maintained, as it was decreed by Pope Pius V in the sixteenth-century, and remains to this day.

Since Easter Monday is the Feast of the Angels at the Holy Sepulchre, Monday is thought of as the day of the angels and the Joyful Mysteries are recited on Monday and again on Thursday. Tuesday, the day of apostles and Friday, the day of the Crucifixion, are the days of the Sorrowful Mysteries.

The Glorious Mysteries are said on three days, on Saturday traditionally the day of Our Lady, Wednesday the day of the Holy Spirit and Sunday the holy day of the week. Many people recite the entire Psalter daily but these are the days that have traditionally been held appropriate to the different subjects.

The origin of many of these devotions is to be found in this country and there is no doubt of their popularity, but it cannot be claimed that they were only in circulation in England.

The monks and abbots who helped to compose them were constantly on the move between the different houses of their orders throughout Europe and many of them came from the great abbey of Cluny in France and the Benedictine network spreading throughout Europe.

St. Anselm, Archbishop of Canterbury came here from Normandy and there were great exponents of Marian devotion in France, notably St. Bernard of Clairvaux who was one of the first to break away from Cluny to join the newly founded Cistercian order, and his writings in the twelfth-century are amongst the most beautiful ever composed on the subject of Our Lady.

In putting forward the notion that the rosary may well have roots in England, there is ample proof that she was truly the dowry of Mary, and that the devotion of the people was noted by their continental neighbours. This view seems to be confirmed by a report on the state of England in 1496 made by a secretary of the Venetian Embassy: "They all hear mass every day, and say many Paternosters (rosaries) in public, the women carrying long strings of beads in their hands and whoever is at all able to read carries with him the Office of Our Lady: and they recite it in Church with some companion in a low voice, verse by verse, after the manner of the religious".[14] He must have felt the sight unusual enough to describe in such detail, almost with a sense of awe.

Throughout the story of the rosary, the figures whose actions affected the subsequent development of the prayer and whose names recur are those of different Dominican monks. Much of the Dominican link with the rosary is prompted by the awareness of the importance of inward calm and recollection in prayer held by St. Dominic and the great strength he drew from it in his struggles with the heretics in the twelfth-century. The Dominicans are the especial custodians of the rosary and St. Dominic is undoubtedly the central figure in the story of Our Lady's Psalter.

CHAPTER THREE

Dominic was his name, whose work and worth
I publish, as the husbandman whom Christ
called to His Garden to help till the earth.

Dante. *The Divine Comedy.* Paradise Canto XII

ST. DOMINIC — *Detail, Fra Angelico. The Museo S. Marco.*

CHAPTER THREE

THE quiet plains between the Tigris and the Euphrates where the rose first bloomed in Mesopotamia was also the birthplace of a preacher named Manes who was born in the third-century. His teaching was to prove the adversary in a fierce struggle for the minds and souls of the people of Languedoc in the twelfth-century whose outcome proved for once and for all the great power of the rosary.

The end of that long drawn out battle marked not only the defeat of a destructive evil but the arrival of the prayer of the rosary, as it emerged from confused and tentative beginnings and became the meditative prayer we have today.

Almost any Catholic will tell you with unwavering certainty that the rosary was founded by St. Dominic, adding something vague about the south of France, but both statements are misleading. There is no evidence that St. Dominic founded or invented the rosary, in fact all the evidence shows that as a means of counting prayers, this little circlet of beads was in use long before St. Dominic appeared on the scene, and yet generations of devotees have clung happily to this belief while those with a detective's taste for facts have given themselves headaches over the whole issue.

Over the centuries, in an attempt to satisfy the sleuths, enthusiastic Dominicans have produced "evidence" of either miracles or certainly extraordinary coincidences, as if to pull a rabbit out of a hat, such as the avalance of roses that is said to have cascaded down upon the victors of the battle of Murat during the Albigensian Crusade.

On another occasion a document was found and said to provide definitive evidence but the eager soul overlooked the difference between the words "Dominus" and "Dominicus" in touching enthusiasm that was bound to exasperate the historian and seeker after proof, with the result that most people dismiss the whole story for dependence on such flimsy evidence.

But perhaps the "learned historians" have their problems too for any visitor to the Church of Santa Maria Novella in Florence will see on peering into the darkness penetrated only by the flickering altar light, the dark forms of devout figures holding beads before a near life-size tableau of Mary, her hands outstretched to give the rosary to St. Dominic, and the sceptic slips softly into the shadows, his scholarship meaningless before the overwhelming power of faith before him nearly eight hundred years after the death of the saint.

For St. Dominic's influence on the development of the rosary was profound and through his teaching this form of prayer its true worth and efficacy were realised for the first time, and it is for this reason that successive Popes have firmly placed the duty of the propagation of the rosary on Dominican shoulders.

The airy reference to the south of France is confusing too, for in the late twelfth-century when these events took place, the area in question was nominally an English province through the marriage of Henry II to Eleanor of Aquitaine, taking its name of Languedoc from the language of the Troubadours in which *oc* instead of *oui* meant yes.

From the Pyrenees along the Mediterranean coast to the Alps in the east the waves on the shore echo the waves of armies that have appeared over her jagged hills, filling the air with battle cries that fade in time to make way for the next conquerors. The Greeks first planted her vineyards and olive groves centuries before Christ, only to make way for the Romans on their victorious path from Italy to find the pride of their Empire, Provincia Romania. A period of great calm followed interrupted only by Hannibal tramping across from Spain with his army and fifty-one elephants, and then he too vanished over the horizon.

Peace was restored until the Romans finally left in the fifth-century to defend the remnants of their Empire, making way for the marauding hordes of Visigoths and Franks two centuries later.

The sea at that time provided a safer passage for traders than the highways, the coastal province of Languedoc was a great meeting place and the streets of Montpellier thronged with Arab, Italian and English traders. A visitor to that coastline today would take the many nationalities for granted and the sounds of wailing sirens and blaring music need little imagination to change to Medieavel sounds filling the dusty air with shouts of traders from Byzantium, Egypt and Syria with their fine clothes and spices.

But to travel into the hills behind the coast is to roll away the centuries. There the villages cling like limpets to bare rocks, their Roman tiled roofs undulating in the sunlight and beneath them, the arches and pools of shadow where children play barefooted in the parched yellow grass that eeks its existence from the baked soil.

Across the vineyards the trees are twisted and contorted by the cruel mistral which blows from the sea to the indigo hills in the distance. The imprint of the Roman is so obvious to see that it seems that only the coastline has succumbed to the webb of successive conquerors, like a young siren lured this way and that in search of new delights that turn sour in the palm, and there is an unmistakably Moorish element in the exotic atmosphere of Languedoc.

In the midst of this idyllic countryside, like a blight that descends on the most flourishing harvest, the Albigensian heresy took root.

The heresy was in fact as old as the hills, and owed its new name to the village of Albi in Languedoc where its followers gathered in strength in the middle of the twelfth-century, and their professed faith was Manicheeism with a new face but an unchanged character.

The teaching of Manes was based on the belief that all matter is evil and that man is a combination of two opposing principles. A spiritual being created by God, thrust into a material body created by an evil being, and the heroes of this strange faith were called the "cathari" or pure ones.

The most serious implication of this teaching was the denial of the two natures of Christ for they refused to accept His Humanity while acknowledging His Divinity, and this in turn led to total rejection of the New Testament and any part of the Old Testament that did not agree with their teaching.

All beauty that surrounds man was seen not as a gift of an indulgent Creator, but as the demonstration of evil from which escape was the only hope. All human love, itself a mirror of God's love, was obscured and abhorred, for it demonstrated to the heretic man's reluctance to banish human ties.

Lives of the utmost austerity and self-denial were led by its followers involving fearful mortifications and beatings to subdue the flesh.

Marriage was forbidden since its purpose was the procreation of children, and therefore the further imprisonment of spirit in matter. The ultimate release from evil was the deliverance of the soul, and if undertaken in the form of suicide this was greatly admired.

Since this way of life was somewhat daunting, and in fact placed the future of the human race in some doubt, the Cathari invented a kind of two tier system. The inner sanctum of the "Perfects" led this rule to the letter, while it was recognised that for lesser mortals who might already be married and leading normal lives, more modest but no less pernicious demands were made. They were required to repudiate the Church, denounce the sacraments and deny the Gospels, and above all, to work for the spread of the heresy.

From our viewpoint eight centuries later, it seems curious that an evil of such harshness could have held attractions and the sweep of its success across the region seems incomprehensible.

However, the monastic orders were past their zenith, and the glories of Cluny were fading. The age that had seen the concentration of all learning within the monasteries, the creation of the most priceless manuscripts and illuminations ever seen, was gone. The means of ensuring the primacy of the Church as the seat of all learning, had become unwittingly the means of accumulating great wealth. The single pursuit of spiritual perfection had become lost as the monastic orders went out into the world to care for their new possessions and the monks became by definition more worldly. The care for their most precious responsibility, the souls of their flocks, became lax and ineffectual.

In a more spiritual age man understood even in this confusion, the unsatisfactory nature of worldly goods and in the brilliant life of the courts of Languedoc where great wealth and indulgence held sway, amidst the revelry there was the uneasy feeling that all was not well. The priests to whom these people turned, half wanting but at least expecting admonishment and the teaching of more lasting values, were themselves too involved in the very things from which others sought escape. The spiritual guidance and forgiveness of sin were not forthcoming and this state of affairs made a fertile seed-bed for the rigours of the heresy.

The wealth of the Church seemed immense and it was not long before envious eyes were turned upon such an Aladdin's cave. The nobles eagerly listened to the fierce strictures of the Manichees fulminating against the property of the Church and the wild promise of land seizure was an irresistible lure to which their followers happily responded.

Although we think of the twentieth-century as the scientific age to end all, when it came to learning, the people of the Middle Ages exhibited a far more scientific turn of mind, and the wheat-germ theories of doing your own thing, or setting out on a voyage of self-discovery would have been incomprehensible and extremely distasteful to them. Theories of a purely logical nature were far more to their liking and the Universities were places where few facts were taught but the students acquired the ability to learn from a basis of logic, grammer and rhetoric. In this sense alone, the deceptively precise nature of the heresy held a fascination.

Lastly, but certainly not least, there was the promise of the "Consolatum", a ceremony which promised the release of the soul to eternal happiness. If timed correctly in the last moments of life, all was well and lives of the utmost chaos and indulgence could be enjoyed until then and Raymond, Count of Toulouse was known to travel everywhere accompanied by a "Perfect" in case death should take him by surprise.

At first, the Church was slow to react and did so only in response to repeated demands from the populace who in many cases took matters into their own hands. The heresy was seen as a threat to society as a whole dividing families and villages in the same way that in our century various freak sects have inflicted immense sufferings on the families of their followers.

However, in the eleventh- and twelfth-centuries, when for many the Church was the State, the Civitas Dei, most were aware of this threat to the very structure of society. The peace and continuity of family life was being disrupted by an alien force, bent on bringing dissention and betrayal, not only by driving its members apart but by attacking the rock on which the family was based.

Initially, the hierarchy seemed content to issue excommunications while the secular authority enforced exile and on occasion the confiscation of property but there were times when an exasperated people acted alone, out of impatience with clerical leniency, and those they considered to be heretics were burned by enraged mobs.

There were some people who with perception understood the nature of the problem, and saw clearly the need to reaffirm the teaching of the Christian faith, often in the face of bitter antagonism.

St. Bernard of Clairvaux left the "Black Monks" to join the Cistercian order with the sole intention of returning to the strict rule of St. Benedict. He travelled the area of Languedoc tirelessly preaching to hostile crowds and on one occasion he was driven to such exasperation that he laid a curse on a village for refusing to allow him speech.

Eventually even he was driven away overwhelmed by the effects of the heresy, the sight of empty churches and unbaptised children, ignored by clergy too indolent to dispense the Sacraments. Yet despite urgent appeals to the contrary, St. Bernard preached persuasion rather than coercion.

These were the rumors carried across the Pyrenees by visitors to the canonry at Osma in 1200 where a young Spaniard was studying in peace and sanctity within the tranquil cloisters, a tranquillity soon to be broken forever, for Dominic de Guzman was laying the spiritual foundation for the immense task that awaited him.

*   *   *   *   *   *   *

St. Dominic was born in Castile, a land long used to producing Christian heroes, but perhaps none so great as he. In a rugged terrain of harsh austerity, the sweeping plains form a barren landscape contrasting sharply with the luxurious growth of flowers and pine woods flourishing along the river beds. In the eleventh- and twelfth-century it formed the frontier of Christian defense against the Moor, its hills topped with stern fortified castles and villages, the last outpost of Christian Spain. St. Dominic was born in the midst of this countryside of noble parents whose record of service to their King and faith was impressive. Yet this stern land was renowned also as the land of ballads where the troubadours sang their plaintive songs and Dante wrote dream-like verses about the strange beauty of the birthplace of the saint.

The formidable traits of heroic courage and chivalry combined with a gentle compassion were reflected in St. Dominic's character. He was said to have been a serious child who grew into a man of ruthless severity with himself, and yet inheriting from his mother Joanna a great love of the poor and for those in need. Through all these different traits there shone a character infused with a love of God that brought a serene joy illuminating his entire life.

Fortunately we have many accounts of St. Dominic's appearance and personality from those who shared his life and work, given at the processs for his canonization which took place less than fifteen years after his death.

His contemporaries describe him as a "strong athlete" of Spanish appearance and strikingly handsome with great dignity of carriage and yet the most humble of men, capable of great physical endurance, whose fine features revealed his strength of purpose. In contrast to this rather daunting picture, these same people tell of his humour and love of music, for he sang with a clear and beautiful voice as he hurried along the dusty roads of France and Spain. His personal austerity was awesome and throughout his life he would eat only bread and water, always insisting on sleeping on rough boards driving to despair those who longed to care for him.

He possessed great equanimity and was very affectionate, and from the gentle pen of his most beloved companion and successor as head of the Order, Jordan of Saxony, comes the most complete account of St. Dominic. The phrases which tell more than mere words can express are short and direct, vivid with the joy and inspiration felt by all who shared his company, reaching undiminished across the centuries. He was always happy on his own account, and only sad out of sympathy with the sufferings of others, "none was ever more joyous than he and none a better companion" are the words of his first biographer.

In the year 1200 he was subprior of Osma having been ordained five years earlier, and in spite of the seclusion of this life of prayer and learning, he was quickly noticed by his fellows and loved for his great charm and prodigious knowledge.

In 1203 he was chosen to accompany his Bishop as a special emissary of the Pope on a visit to the Marches, and on their return from this journey the two passed through Languedoc for the first time. While they rested overnight in Toulouse, Dominic fell into conversation with their innkeeper who had recently abandoned his faith and joined the Albigenses. The dispute raged all night until by morning the exhaused publican, overcome by the persuasions of the fiery young priest, repented and returned to the Church.

This was the unlikely beginning of St. Dominic's life of preaching, and, combined with the arrival on the scene of one of the greatest statesmen of mediaeval Europe, Pope Innocent III a few years earlier, marked the first steps towards the eventual defeat of the Albigensian heresy.

St. Dominic soon returned to Languedoc, and became a familiar sight travelling the length and breadth of the area, preaching tirelessly in one village before hurrying on to the next. Others came to join him, not as yet bound to each other by the rules of an order, but united in their will to bring the word of God, in all its lucid purity, to anyone who would listen.

Meanwhile, since 1198 the Papal legates had trodden a continuous path from Rome to Toulouse, some becoming increasingly overwhelmed by their task to the point where they begged the Pope to be allowed to return to the seclusion of their monasteries.

Those who did venture forth to face taunting crowds were few and the sight that greeted the onlooker was startling. Long processions of lurching carriages wound through the dusty heat bearing the monks, who gazed with melancholy eye on the indifferent villagers while they paused to address in stentorian tones those who would listen, before the whole sorry caravan moved on to the next village. The contrast between this spectacle and the sight of their new Albigensian "saviours" with their long faces of self-denial prompting loud groans of admiration, spoke oceans and needless to say the monks met with little success. The Pope was driven to saying bitterly that they were "watchdogs who have lost their bark" and "hirelings who abandon their flock to the wolves".

This was the sight that greeted St. Dominic and his followers on their travels. The anguish they felt at the sight of men abandoning their vocations was almost greater than the pity they felt for the flock so casually abandoned, for in their sorry state, the clergy were more demoralized than corrupt and their preaching, such as it was, had been reduced to hazy admonishment. This sorry state of affairs revealed an underlying flaw in the training of these men, for there was a breakdown in the old organization of European education which was a cause of concern to the Church and of hope to her enemies.

St. Dominic was thirty-three years old when he reached Languedoc. The next seventeen years were spent in ceaseless endeavour establishing his order of preachers who were to go to the Universities and become the foremost teachers of the age. Eventually his order would travel to the four corners of the world, teaching the words of Christ not with loud denunciations but with brilliantly reasoned interpretation of the truths of the faith in words for all to understand.

In 1206 all that lay in the future as St. Dominic prepared for his mission in Toulouse. He realised the need for clear teaching above all, and he and his followers quickly rejected the indolent luxury of the monasteries. Their own self-inflicted austerity, travelling bare footed and in abject poverty from village to village, earned the reluctant admiration of the heretics.

In 1208 Peter of Castelnau, the Pope's legate, was murdered as he crossed the Rhone near Arles one evening and this signalled the beginning of a war whose aims became increasingly confused. At times it was far more territorial and political than religious as various factions seized the opportunity to settle feudal disputes and to take vast areas of land they had long coveted.

The Crusade, launched by Pope Innocent III, set out in 1208 led by Christian forces from all over Europe. Despite some successes which included the miraculous deliverance and victory against overwhelming forces at the walls of Muret in 1213, there were horrifying deeds of violence and brutality on both sides, and the Crusade finally exhausted itself in 1215 with the death of its leader, Simon de Montfort.

Throughout the Crusade, St. Dominic witnessed the carnage with growing disquiet and made efforts to separate himself from those involved, for the fervour with which the heretics were struck down was difficult to reconcile with Christianity.

St. Dominic always took the opportunity to enter any church he was passing, for the chance to speak with his Lord was irresistible to the saint. On one of these occasions, tradition has decreed that Our Lady appeared to him in the church of Notre Dame de la Dreche. To comfort him in his sadness, the Blessed Virgin gave St. Dominic her especial prayer of the rosary, with the instruction that this prayer should be offered by the people as an antidote to heresy.

The validity of this scene has been subjected to the most vigorous scrutiny down the centuries, and although not formally acknowledged by the Church, many wise heads have happily accepted the apparition of Notre Dame de la Dreche as a most apt beginning for the prayer of the rosary. Certainly it was apt that this saint should be credited by many with the founding of the rosary not perhaps for any dramatic deed on his part, but because the study of the life of St. Dominic is in itself the perfect study of the prayer of the rosary, and his example gives us some understanding of the prayer Our Lady, on behalf of her Son, demands from us.

Sometimes it is felt that Dominic must have been in need of gentle admonishment for the length of his erudite sermons, and a reminder of the importance of prayer, but that is the reaction of ordinary mortals; his whole personality was infused with a deep contemplative spirituality that lesser beings could scarcely begin to conceive.

Of all people, he understood that truth needs no embellishment, that wisdom like the light that illuminates the world, is to be gained in understanding and not in rhetoric, and that understanding is only given through the power of prayer and meditation in the true silence of the soul. The foundation of that knowledge had been laid during his nine years in the peace of Osma in Spain long before he reached Languedoc.

His prayer consisted of long periods of contemplation interrupted only by moments of speech, almost as if he were involved in deep conversation with his Lord. Sometimes his monks would see him thus in wrapt attention on occasion with his head to one side as if listening intently to someone who was addressing words of profound importance to him.

His love of prayer, usually sung, was infectous and he would exhort his friars to greater efforts with the words *fortiter fratres* as he paced along their choir stalls. Above all, the reciting of the Office afforded time for the prolonged contemplation of the mysteries and words of God. Anything that brought Christ more vividly to his mind was eagerly grasped and dwelt upon, such as the Sacraments or the beads of a rosary.

In his beautiful book, *The Life of St. Dominic* Father Bede Jarrett says, "It was for this reason that the devotion of the rosary found in him its keenest apostle. His own way of prayer consisting as we have seen of vocal expressions of love and adoration, was intermingled with silences; it passed from speech to contemplation as it fixed itself on to the character of Our Lord. All these elements were united in the rosary. It was contemplative and vocal."

The clearest illustration we have of this unearthly knowledge and familiarity with the life of the Saviour is portrayed by Fra Angelico whose paintings seem like small windows to heaven.

Sceptics have often pointed out that if St. Dominic was indeed handed the rosary by the Blessed Virgin, surely of all subjects Fra Angelico would have found this one irresistible, and yet not once did he appear to find time to do so. This misses the point, and like so many human reactions it needs turning upside down to reach the real answer.

The Dominicans became above all the preachers of the Church. Following the example of St. Dominic, great knowledge, a dry and dusty commodity on its own, was to be distilled and brought to fruition by the power of prayer. St. Dominic enveloped his monks in an austere spirituality with strict rules of chastity, obedience and poverty not to draw acclaim from others in the manner of the Albigenses, but to inflame their hearts with the love of God. Their rhetoric as they travelled around the Universities of Europe was undoubtedly intellectually inspiring, but it was above all wisdom directed by prayer.

The events in the life of Christ and the example set by the life of the Holy Family described in the New Testament, were the complete denial of the tenets of the Albigensian heretics, whose bitter diatribes of hatred were in sharp contrast to the flowing words of the Dominicans which were deepened by a true spirituality. Thus the Dominican insistence on meditation together with gentle repetitive words of adoration was given to the world as the example for the Christian to follow, and as the antedote to all heresy. That prayer we have come to know as the rosary.

The life of austerity and prayer became the inspiration to action and St. Dominic insisted on the most rigorous study from his followers. His love of learning and logic were legendary and books were the only luxury in an otherwise awesome simplicity allowed to his friars. These things were to be treasured not in themselves, but as the essential weapons of a life devoted to preaching. One chronicler of the time noted that as the saint travelled to and fro across the war-torn plains of Languedoc he was seen always with staff and book in hand.

When studying as a young man at Valencia, a great drought brought hardship and starvation to the farming people of the area, and Dominic, overwhelmed with compassion, sold all his books to help them. He seems to have made a habit of impulsively shedding all his books with the result that he developed the ability to store wisdom within himself, thereby meditating on the matter of his reading and storing within a contemplative mind great tomes of knowledge. He made no secret of his wish to attract the most brilliant minds of the time to his order, for in an age that was alive with speculation, he realized the need for lucid and exhaustive study.

However, his prodigious intellect had its drawbacks, for he never found need to commit any of his sermons to paper, and we have to rely on the accounts of those who heard him at the time, preaching in the sunbaked fields or village squares of Languedoc. Those who witnessed these scenes were moved either to anguish or joy by the gentle insistence of that clear Castilian voice, and "people were glad to hear him" is the simple verdict of one who was there.

In the course of his teaching St. Dominic preached the form of prayer we recognize as the rosary. The division into fifteen different subjects on which to dwell, each one a different event in the life of Our Lord and the Blessed Virgin, combined with a suitable devotion, enabled him to instruct with clarity those who gathered to hear him. Though the prayer was never specifically named by St. Dominic or those immediately around him, we have the evidence of one of his friars who joined the order during the life time of the saint, and on whose prayer he undoubtedly modelled his own. Mention has already been made of Romeus de Livia, who was in the custom of meditating on the Blessed Virgin and the Child Jesus whilst reciting his Aves counted with the aid of a knotted cord.

As the year 1215 progressed, the purpose of the Crusade gradually became buried in conflicting violence, for the lenient terms of agreement set by the Pope served only to encourage the Albigeois to interpret such reason as a sign of weakness, and lack of confidence in the leadership of Simon de Montfort. St. Dominic alarmed at the menace to his new order, returned to Prouille with his sixteen followers. After receiving their professions and blessing them, he explained his intention of dispersing his flock, "hoarded the grain rots; cast it to the winds it brings forth fruit."

Women too played an important part in St. Dominic's work. Their adherence to his teaching became one of the great achievements of his ministry, and in fact his first religious house was founded for women.

One summer's evening in 1206, while the saint sat reading outside the gates of Fanjeaux, he looked across the valley in the fading evening light towards the line of black mountains in the distance. There he saw descending from heaven a globe of flame which hovered over the church of Prouille, and to this day the hill is known as the "signadou" the sign from God, and it is here that he founded his first convent whose inhabitants were women converted from amongst the "perfects" of the heresy. They were devoted to him, and Sister Cecilia for one gives a glowing account of the saint in these words, "he was always radiant and joyous except when moved to compassion by some misfortune or other of his neighbours". There is a touching description of his return on foot from Rome when on one occasion he brought back for each of his beloved sisters a small wooden spoon.

A rare glimpse of his humour is shown in a remark that he made to his biographer Jordan of Saxony in whom he confided his preference for speaking with young rather than old women, a passage that was deleted by the general Chapter of 1242.

It is sad that today St. Dominic is so often identified with the Inquisition and little else. The first Inquisition was a secular affair and was set up several years before his time, for heresy was considered to be a crime against society. As time went on, the legal wrangles became increasingly acrimonious and the Inquisition became the means for some of removing political and personal enemies. Eventually the Church stepped in to remove the trial of heretics to the ecclesiastical courts but this was not until ten years after the death of St. Dominic.

When the Dominicans were directed by the Pope to undertake this final act against the heretics, they were extremely reluctant to do so and the Pope eventually commanded their obedience. Dominic's own life bore testimony to his dislike of force as a means of saving souls and this was emphasized by his disenchantment with the Crusade. For the weapons of his personal war were spiritual and intellectual. On only one occasion was he known to have been present at the burning of heretics and then according to Theodoric of Alpodia he rescued one of the victims from the flames. At the same time he displayed a quiet strength of purpose that never faltered and his love of God and hatred for the workings of the heresy engulfed his entire life.

The years between 1215 and 1221 saw the saint continually on the move, organizing his various provinces, teaching without cease and praying at all times, especially when at last alone at the end of the day, when others had taken refuge in sleep.

Eventually in a state of exhaustion, he was overcome by fever when visiting Bologna in 1221. In an attempt to find relief for their saint from the heat of the city, his friars carried him up to the church of St. Mary of the Hills. There he lay for several days in the cool beneath the terraces of vine, reflecting on his life and instructing his grieving brethren on the labours that lay ahead of them.

Finally realizing that death was near, he asked that he be taken back to Bologna for he wished to be in the midst of his brotherhood, and there as they prayed together, he died on Friday, August 6, 1221.

The process for his canonization started only fifteen years after his death. During the time of his successor Jordon of Saxony the work of preaching found one of its greatest teachers, Albert of Cologne, whose student, St. Thomas Aquinas, completed the work started by St. Dominic a century earlier, with a great shout of "that will settle the Manichees" before the entire court of the King of France.

St. Dominic's name is linked irradicably with the rosary and in a spiritual sense he was indeed the true founder of this prayer. Through the power of this small circlet of beads more was wrought than ever the sword could achieve, and that simple message of few words but profound meaning remains true to this day.

CHAPTER FOUR

"All night she sat in bidding of her bedes
And all day in doing good and Godly deeds."

Spencer's Faerie Queen

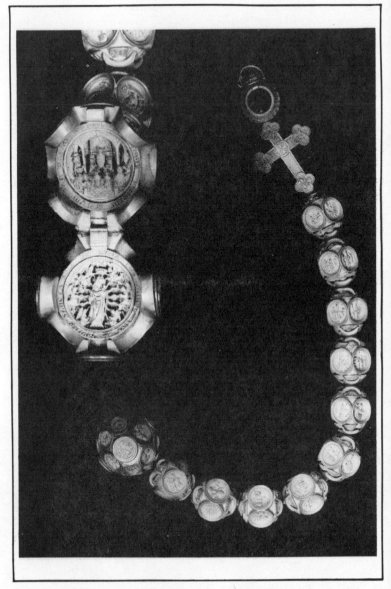

THE ROSARY OF KING HENRY VIII — Known as the Chatsworth Rosary, Devonshire Collection, Chatsworth. *Reproduced by permission of the Chatsworth Settlement Trustees.*

CHAPTER FOUR

THE Dominican order spread rapidly. In 1221, the year of his death, St. Dominic sent twelve friars to England where they were greeted in Canterbury by Stephen Langton, then Archbishop. From there they travelled on foot to Oxford arriving on the Feast of the Assumption to establish themselves east of St. Aldate where they built a chapel to Our Lady.

Almost immediately the work of preaching was started and throughout the surrounding countryside the Dominicans became a familiar sight as they travelled from village to village gathering small crowds around them as people laid down their work to listen. Undoubtedly they preached the prayer of the rosary if not by that name yet, at least in the form to which St. Dominic attached so much importance, namely the contemplation of the events of the New Testament combined with the recitation of prayer. There is little doubt that this form of prayer was already familiar in the monasteries and probably to the communities in their immediate neighbourhood and the "black friars" went out into the fields and byeways preaching the right of everyone, not merely those of the religious life, to this "Little Office". Their labours met with great success for by the end of the thirteenth-century prayer beads had arrived and they aroused such enthusiasm that even the monks were taken by surprise and eventually they found cause to frown.

During the next century the growing popularity of the beads was not merely one of religious associations alone, and jewellers enjoyed a hayday as they explored endless possibilities for the use of precious stones and metals. Some of the descriptions of rosaries of the period read like tales from Aladdin's cave, and the makers of beads seemed happy to go to any lengths to satisfy the whims and fancies of the day. In the event they unwittingly added fuel to the flames of Lutheran disapproval and the hurricane of reform that ensued.

The next two centuries in England are interesting because it was during this time that rosaries became familiar objects and this familiarity ran riot as nearly everyone sought not only to possess a rosary but in many cases to have a bigger and better one than his neighbour, until the Reformation put a stop to any such gaiety. By that time the prayer of the rosary and prayer beads were such an integral part of the life of a Catholic that their suppression was most acutely felt, and men were to die, stubbornly refusing to submit to that suppression.

These were the years of the development of the rosary, a time that saw its tentative arrival followed by a period of acceptance, and an awareness of great spiritual value that threatened eventually to be eclipsed by luxury, and the events that affected that process are worthy of attention.

The word bead comes from the Saxon verb "bidden" to invite or pray, so that originally to "bid the beads" meant simply to say one's prayers, for the word bede meant prayer. Gradually the word bede, beade or bead came to refer to the small circle of wood or whatever material it was, for it represented a prayer and so the word was quite appropriate. Not until the end of the sixteenth-century was all religious association removed, and the round sphere through which a chain was threaded to form a necklace retained the earlier name.

The use of beads as a numonic device was by no means the exclusive right of the Christian. The Crusaders had already discovered Muslims using exotic counting beads, and some writers seem to find a definite link between the appearance of prayer beads in Europe in the twelfth- and thirteenth-centuries and the Crusades to the Holy Land. In 1272 a monumental slab was carved to decorate the tomb of one crusader, Frere Gerars of the Knights Templar in Liege and he is portrayed with beads in hand.

At the same time, Marco Polo was encountering the King of Malibu on his travels and discovering that the King ". . . wears also, hanging in front of his chest, from the neck downwards, a fine silk thread strung with 104 large pearls and rubies of great price. A reason why he wears this cord with 104 great pearls and rubies is (according to what they tell) that every day, morning and evening he has to say 104 prayers to his idols such is their religion and their custom." (*Marco Polo*. Yules edition II, page 275).

Some three centuries later, St. Francis Xavier was surprised to find that rosaries were familiar to the Buddhists of Japan, but for the Christian the search to find a means of keeping tally with his prayers had begun centuries earlier when the first monk hermit, St. Paul, left his home in Egypt and fled from the confusion of the world. There in the desert he found shelter in a cave used previously by the money makers of Cleopatra's time, and near his new home there flowed a spring beneath a palm tree, thus as the story of his life neatly comments, he was provided with drink and clothing. While time and custom carry him light years from today, his longing to find some means of counting his prayers and thereby gaining a sense of achievement are familiar enough, and he gathered each day three hundred pebbles which he passed through his fingers as he prayed.

His first life was written by another hermit of the desert, St. Jerome, of whom there is a portrait in the National Gallery. He is portrayed seated on a rock in the desert praying and fingering a primitive circle of beads while a lion sleeps peacefully by his feet.

In their solitude, time can have had little reality or importance and these simple means of counting provided anchors of stability in a life that threatened to dissolve in a haze of light and sanctity, and evidence has been found that these simple devices were carried to the grave.

Such were the means of keeping a tally of prayers until the eleventh-century. Europe then awoke from a century of Viking invasion to the time of greatest glory in the history of the monasteries, and the focus of this achievement was the great monastery of Cluny in France. In the words of one of the first monks, "it was a valley shut off from all contact, which breathed such a perfume of aloofness, repose and peace, that it seemed like a heavenly solitude". In the midst of this heavenly solitude the abbey of Cluny was built and within its pale walls the community lived in strict observance of the Rule laid down by St. Benedict four centuries earlier.

The community that gathered in this renowned centre of Western monasticism was made up of monks and lay brethren known as the *conversii*. The monks remained for the most part within the abbey, leading a life devoted to the liturgy and the constant search for sanctity prescribed by the Rule while the *conversii* undertook the practical and domestic duties of the monastery. However, all attended the daily recital of the office laid down by St. Benedict and this included the recital of the 150 Psalms. The lay brethren or *conversii* were usually illiterate and to memorize the entire Psalter was beyond them. To enable them to take part in the prayer of the community they were allowed to recite the appropriate number of Paternosters with the help of a knotted string. People from the neighbouring villages summoned by the great Monastery bell followed the example of the *conversii*, and thus was launched with practical simplicity the tradition of reciting 150 prayers with the aid of a string of beads, or in this case, knots.

Because prayers were originally counted in this way, prayer beads were often referred to as a "pair of Paternosters" or simply "Paternosters" and the people who recited them were referred to as "Paternosterers". The gentle sound of their repetitive prayer has often been cited as the source of our expression "pitter-patter".

The peace and holiness of Cluny became the inspiration for great learning and the monks restored much of the knowledge damaged or abandoned during the dark centuries leading up to their own. Their exquisite illuminations awakened a longing for and a recognition of beauty and their influence was widespread.

In 1041 soon after the founding of Cluny, we read from the writings of William of Malmesbury in England that Lady Ghodiva was bequeathing a "circle of threaded jewels upon which she was wont to number her prayers, to be hung about the neck of the Blessed Virgin's image in the church at Coventry". This was long before St. Dominic could have "invented" the rosary, and so it is safe to assume that Lady Ghodiva only used her jewelled beads to count her prayers, and yet the instruction that her beads be bequeathed to the statue of Mary implies a devotion and gratitude for favours received. As this coincided with a spread of devotion to Our Lady in Europe, it therefore seems likely that the prayers she counted were Ave Marias, and not the Paternoster as was the custom.

One of the effects of the Cluniac influence was that from the twelfth-century until the end of the fifteenth, art was looked upon as one of several forms of worship and as a visual addition to man's understanding of the scriptures. Most of the illuminations and masterpieces created before the Renaissance are the work of anonymous monks who looked beyond this world for their reward. Their sense of proportion and humility dictated that time spent in such labour was immaterial, and hour after hour, year in year out, the laborious and exquisite work progressed as a continual prayer. With great love and painstaking attention, glowing borders of jewel like flowers and birds were painted on parchment to surround the faces of the saints; art for art's sake in the complete sense of the word. When old age and infirmity eventually slowed the hand at work, the aged monk handed his pens and brushes to a younger man who took up the task. Such things as deadlines or the vagaries of a fickle patron were totally unknown to him.

The effect on the laity was obvious and it is hard for us in the twentieth-century to understand the volume of output in works of art which were created for the glory of God. All the artistic energy which is today poured into creating songs or films was in the days of Cluniac influence directed solely towards the embellishment of the liturgy, the illumination of priceless manuscripts or the architecture of great abbeys; rosaries were not left out of this new awareness and they became increasingly beautiful.

Seen in this light, the jewelled beads of the time fit quite naturally into an overall picture of the exuberant worship of God, for all this activity came before the pall of Puritan austerity had descended, when all that was grey and severe was considered fit for a God Who in return gave man a world of light and beauty.

Thus the rosary beads were added to the luggage of the Christian pilgrim, and they became the object of attention as if seen for the first time in the new light of discovery. Not only were beads of practical use, but as they assisted the quantity of prayer so the quality of this renewed fervour was reflected in more tangible form. Beads became not simply knots of twine, but jewels strung on exquisite threads of gold fit for a king's ransom.

In this respect Christian beads bore an uncanny resemblance to those beads of other cultures and religions, but for all that they were different. The reason lay not so much in their ornate quality but in the manner in which they differed from other prayer beads which had been in use before them; the great beads of the King of Malibu or the strange and exotic beads seen by the Crusaders to the lands of Saladin in the East, and that essential difference lay in matters spiritual. For the beads of a Catholic are blessed by a priest and as such they become an instrument of grace in direct relationship to the person for whom they are blessed. There is a prayer from the Old Sarum rite which was used in Saxon England for the blessing of beads which includes the words: "Whoever endeavours by means of these (beads) to honour by holy service the most Blessed Mary, Mother of God, may her Son our Lord Jesus Christ return him great things for small; may He accept his devotion, forgive him his sins, fill him with faith, indulgently succour him, mercifully protect him, destroy whatever is adverse to him, and grant him what is prosperous."

The importance of the individual in relation to the beads that are blessed is underlined by an incident that occurred at Lourdes during the apparitions of Our Lady to St. Bernadette in 1860. There was in St. Bernadette's class a girl who wished her rosary to be blessed by "the Lady" and she entreated Bernadette to exchange her beads when next she visited the grotto. With misgivings

Bernadette did so. When Our Lady appeared she hesitated and her lips move, "That is not your rosary" she murmured. Bernadette explained and the vision receded, saying "where is your own?" Bernadette hastily turned and grasped her own beads from the hands of her friend.

There could be no clearer instruction from a more august source of the importance attached to the beads themselves. No other article has been singled out for such attention and it is an indication of the power for acquiring grace and spiritual happiness which is encompassed by this ring of beads, and the great joy to Mary when this prayer is recited in her honour.

This sense of reverence is underlined by the custom in many countries of people being buried with their beads resting in their hands. In the days when great monuments were carved on the tombs of the deceased it was quite usual that the adornment of the figure should include a rosary.

In the Monumenta Vestuta there is a plate showing an effigy of Richard Patten carrying at his waist a purse, a dagger and a rosary, being thus ready for anything.[1] One of the oldest examples of this custom is to be seen in Paris on the tombstone of the Dauphin Humbertus who became a Dominican and died in 1354, in which two of the Dominicans included in the carving carry rosaries.

The fourteenth-century has been called the calamitous century and in all the turbulence, chroniclers seem to have found little time for gentle ruminations on prayer beads, but events were taking place that were to have far reaching effects on the years to come. The Hundred Years War between England and France brought as a side effect a sense of nationalism dividing the old European unity which meant so much to Catholicism. The Black Death swept through Europe wreaking devastation on the population and in Montpellier alone, of St. Dominic's 140 monks only seven survived, and such was the feeling of despair that one Irish monk wrote: "I leave parchment for continuing the work if any of the race of Adam survive this pestilence."

The great chronicler Froissart appears as immune to human suffering as any journalist for he remarked briefly that "a third of the world died." In Paris it was noted that swearing and gambling had diminshed to such an extent that those engaged in the making of dice were turning their products into beads for "telling Paternosters". Whether to increase their profits or to benefit their souls it is hard to say.

In England the effects of the plague were equally devastating and the effect on the monastic orders was dramatic, greatly reducing their numbers while the monasteries retained the wealth of their scholarship and stewardship had unwittingly gathered. All these seemingly unrelated events were profoundly to affect the years that lay ahead, but the immediate future seemed to bring a temporary calm and a respite in the remorseless train of events, and with it an air of near frivolity.

Wooden beads were once more forgotten while the popularity of ornate rosaries seemed to know no bounds. To cater for the flourishing new industry, the bead-makers installed themselves in London in the shadow of St. Paul's Cathedral and the streets became known as Pater Noster Row and Ave Maria Lane. A London jeweller of the time, one Adam Ledyard, had in his stock Paternoster beads of white and yellow amber, coral, jet and silver, and Ave beads of jet and blue glass as well as cheaper sets of maple and white bone for children. Meanwhile in Paris business was equally brisk for there were three guilds of bead makers each specializing in different materials. It is interesting to note that all the amber which was so popular was supplied solely by the Knights Templar from their vast estates in East Prussia.

Much criticism has been heaped on the immense fortunes spent on ecclesiastical adornment in the Middle Ages and the whole question of opulence versus simplicity is a vexed one. In a sense, each age produces different reactions which vary according to the prevailing sense of values. In the Middle Ages, people clearly understood that prayer was more powerful than money, and material comfort was scarcely considered for it was little enjoyed

even by the wealthy. Man appears to have paid far more attention
to his soul than his body and evidently found it entirely satisfying
to do so, for it remained the norm until the reformation. They
took to heart the words of the Gospel, that "where your heart is,
there also will be your treasure." Since their interest lay in God
and His Church, it seemed appropriate that their efforts should be
concentrated in that direction.

The view was held that the spiritual welfare of a man was his
first consideration and a trouble free life was a gift of a benevolent
God. This emphasis on the importance of the spiritual life is born
out of wills of the time, when much time and thought is given to
spiritual matters, and practical considerations of property are
treated as afterthoughts with great expedience.

The will of Sir Thomas Wyndham in 1521 is a typical example.
After exhorting at great length those who remained to pray for
his soul he makes elaborate and lengthy arrangements for 1000
masses to be said at different times, and in different chapels. Only
after all spiritual matters have been considered, does he turn
briefly to the distribution of his property. Sometimes their wills
show a commendable ingenuity in mixing the practical and sacred
in one instruction. When the Alderman of York died in 1506 he
granted his house to his wife as long as she remained unmarried,
and held each year at Candlemass a dinner for thirteen men and
one woman, "in honor of Christ and His twelve apostells and ye
woman in ye worshippe of oure Ladye and to kepe our Lady
Masse wekely on ye Saturday."[2]

It becomes obvious that prayer, and often prayer in the form of
the rosary, is one of the greatest concerns of a man's life, and therefore beads ranked high in the list of beloved possessions to be handed
down and often they were treated as heirlooms by the recipient.

The families of Yorkshire are happily well documented and the
examples are too numerous to list. One family in particular offers
a glowing example not only for the beauty of their wills but for
the finely detailed portrait that emerges of a noble and Christian
family of England of the time.

In 1401, Richard Scrope, Lord of Bolton, left his son a "pair of paternosters of coral" and two years later his kinsman Roger Lord Scrope left to his son and heir "my pair of Paternosters of coral with a jewel of gold which belonged to my lord, my father; also a cross of gold which I usually carry about with me".[3] In 1451 Lord John Scrope asks in his will that "24 poor men clothed in white gowns and hoods each of them having a new set of wooden beads" should pray on them at his funeral at Scrope's chapel within the Cathedral of York. He adds that these poor men may stand or sit at will. This request is not as strange as it might appear for it was quite common for people to pay others to bid their beads for them particularly when they required all fifteen decades to be said daily, and these people were referred to as bedesmen. Sometimes they too were left money in gratitude for services rendered during the lifetime of the deceased.

In 1488 Agnes, daughter of Lord Scrope, was left by her mother-in-law "a pare of bedes of golde", and in 1498 the will of Lady Anne Scrope sparkles with the jewels she carefully leaves to members of her family and household. One of her rosaries (she leaves three others of coral) is of sufficient value to merit breaking into decades illustrating the sad fate that befell nearly all the priceless beads of the time: "To the rood of North door (St. Paul's in London) my heart with gold with diamond in the midst. To Our Lady of Walsingham 10 of my great beads of gold and tasselled with the same. To Our Lady of Peue (Westminster) 10 of the same beads. To St. Edmund of Bury 10 of the same beads. To St. Thomas of Canterbury, 10 of the same beads. To Thomas Fincham 10 Aves and 2 Paternosters of the same beads."[4]

Other wills offer examples of the strange habit, in our eyes, of bequeathing clothing to various shrines as well as beads, but that is to misunderstand the purpose of such gifts, for many of the ornate vestments of the period were made from such bequests. Thus the will of Dame Catherine Hastings must have been greatly valued: "To Our Lady of Doncaster my tawny chamlett gown. To Our Lady of Belcrosse my black chamlett. To Our Lady of

Hymmymburgh a pece of cremell, and a lace of gold of Venyss
sett wt perle. To my moder my best bedes. To my sister Marger-
ette a pare of beides of whitt jasper. To my neice Agnes a pare of
beides of coral".[5]

Some wills are more obviously practical and to the point like
that of Nicholas Aglionby of 1505: "I bequeth to old John Chap-
man my carlill dagger and a pare of bedes of yalow box."[6]

One of the remarkable facts to be gleaned from these wills is
the apparent variety of stones used by jewellers of the time. Silver
and silver gilt emerge as the most popular metals for the chain and
often the Paternoster bead of gaud as it was often called, as in the
will of Dame Joan Chamberleyn who leaves "a payr of coral
baydes gaudiett wt silver" and Dame Agnes Clifton who leaves
"my sonne's daughter a pare of rown curiall bedes gaudiett wt
silver gilt".

Gold was also popular, as in the rosary John of Gaunt leaves:
"A chain of gold of the old manner with the name of God in each
part, which my most honoured lady and mother the Queen,
whom God pardon, gave me, commanding me to preserve it,
with her blessing; and I desire that he (his son Henry, later King
Henry IV) will keep it, with the blessing of God and mine."[7].

Charles the Bold was said to have inherited some thirty-five
rosaries of coral, crystal, gold and endless other precious jewels
and the makers appear to have been carried away on a tide of
richesse.[8]

Although seen in the kindest light, on most occasions the intention was to make this instrument of prayer as beautiful in
material terms as they wished the prayer to be spiritually, it is difficult not to feel on some occasions that they overdid things. The
Princess Elector of Brandenburg had in her dowry a Paternoster
of gold set with pearls, rubies, emeralds and diamonds, much to
the envy of the English ladies of the court. Some were made of
coral which was said to bring good luck and others were of an immense length. In 1488 the King of Scotland inherited from his
father the "grete bedis" of 122 beads and a tassel, all of gold.[9]

Add to this great size the growing habit of attaching all manner of brooches, rings and cameos, it is a wonder that they did not project themselves into the next life by falling over their rosaries.

Chaucer remarked on this new habit of attachments in his description of the Prioress:

> She wore a trinket on her arm
> A set of beads, the gaudes tricked in green
> Whence hung a golden brooch of brightest sheen
> On which there first was graven a crowned A
> And lower: Amor vincit omnia.[10]

Some time later, Sir Thomas More was obviously amused by the new fashion for in his apologue of the wolf who went to confession to the hypocritical fox he says "his confessor shook his great pair of beads upon him almost as big as bowls."[11]

While all this exuberance held sway, the actual prayer of the rosary was in danger of sinking without trace, and counting the beads threatened to become a profitable pastime in financial rather than spiritual terms. Rosaries which had initially been an "outward sign", had slipped into the culture of the time, with strange and diverse roles ranging from being an essential part of a wedding trousseau, to becoming a status symbol as a gift, and eventually being worn in every way possible, including as a necklace.

When all hope of a return to the real purpose of prayer beads appeared almost lost, there came on the scene a fiery Dominican from Brittany named Alanus de Rupe who made it his main purpose in life to restore the prayer of the rosary. Taking one glance at the situation and using what was to become typically picturesque language, he exhorted his fellow preachers to be like "Noahs making an ark for their brethren" and "Jacobs raising ladders to heaven" and in 1475 with another Dominican Joseph Sprenger, he founded the Confraternity of the Rosary. So great an impact did this man make that while some regarded him as a hot-head and a trouble-maker and others as a saint, many people felt that he was the true founder of the rosary since it was he who made known the apparition of Our Lady to St. Dominic so many years before.

There is little doubt that his preaching was persuasive and the popularity of the Confraternity of the Rosary spread rapidly throughout Europe. Membership entailed no rigours other than the promise to recite the rosary each week, endorsing the promise by signing a book of enrollment and it quickly sought and received papal approval.

The tragedy was that there were not more like him, for by the second half of the fifteenth-century every Catholic who was alive to the situation was clamouring for reform. However they were overtaken by events which even the most pessimistic of their number could not have foreseen.

In England the effects of the Reformation are well known and with hindsight it is possible to fix precise dates, while in practice events unravelled gradually and the unexpected forced awareness.

An ironic example of this is provided by William More, Prior of Worcester. In 1530 Lady Sandys, a favorite of Henry VIII sent William a "peyer of grete amber bedes of 5 settes". She proved a loyal friend for later she wrote to Cromwell on his behalf when More was under house arrest for treason. He was in trouble again some years later for his great extravagance.

But this charge of extravagance became an overworked scapegoat for what followed and the overall image of a Church weighed down by material wealth was used as reason enough for what amounted to legalised vandalism and much of English heritage was destroyed in the effort.

Until his meeting with Anne Boleyn, Henry VIII was known for his great devotion and loyalty to Rome, and the shrine of Our Lady of Walsingham in particular was visited several times by the King. In 1510 he went there on pilgrimage walking the last stage of the journey barefooted, and he presented the statue of Our Lady with a valuable necklace.

It is said that years later as he lay dying he was overheard praying to Our Lady of Walsingham. His rosary is of particular interest because of its intricate composition. Like many prayer beads carried by men it consisted of one decade only and the ten

Aves and one Paternoster hung from his belt. Made in fine box-wood, the Paternoster beads opens to reveal an intricately carved scene from the Mass of St. Gregory with the Virgin and Child enthroned in glory, the same bead being carved with the king's name and royal arms. Known as the Chatsworth rosary, it can be seen today at the home of the Duke of Devonshire.

While Henry laid waste the monasteries of England, his uncle by marriage, the Holy Roman Emperor was battling with the reformers in the Netherlands. Charles V was a man of great holiness and in complete contrast to the custom in England, he carried a simple rosary of wooden beads as a sign of his humility. The wars increased and overwhelmed him to such an extent that he eventually hurried away to a monastery to escape the complexities which he offloaded on to his son Philip II.

With the marriage of Philip to Mary Tudor, there was great hope in England for a return for the old faith but in the event this turned out to be shortlived.

As beads had of old been a sign of penance when worn by pilgrims, so now they became a different sort of sign; William Cecil, the architect of the reformation under Henry VIII is said to have averted the fury of Mary Tudor by parading his prayer beads before the Queen. Another account describes Mary Tudor riding through the city of London and "After her threescore of gentlemen and ladies everyone havying a payre of bedes of black" and on another occasion she purchased a "Payre of bedes of gold enamelled black and white."[12] The beadmakers of Paternoster Lane breathed again. Alas, not for long, for the days when the monks frowned disapprovingly on the laity with their dazzling prayer beads were gone forever.

The reformers themselves unwittingly underlined the importance and sanctity of rosary beads for the mere possession was enough to forfeit a man's life. In the reign of Elizabeth I one Thomas Atkinson was convicted of being a priest on the sole evidence of beads found in his possession and he was taken to York and hanged, drawn and quartered. He was over seventy years of age at the time.

A new type of rosary was needed that took little space, freed from the rhythmic clicking of beads and immediate recognition.

The Knights of Malta wore a form of rosary ring on their sword belts and it was this ring that found its way into use in England during the persecutions. The rosary ring is a small cogwheel with ten knobs for the Aves and a cross for the Paternoster and Gloria. It is easily worn on a finger and turned by the thumb and has been used over the years by Catholics in wartime.

There is however one fine rosary left to us from those troubled times. When Mary Queen of Scots was led to her death in 1587 she carried in her hand her golden rosary, until her executioner stepped forward to claim his traditional right to the adornments of the condemned. Her servant Jane Kennedy protested and on the Queen's plea, the rosary was saved. Jane Kennedy eventually gave it to the Queen's friend Anne Dacre wife of Philip Earl of Arundel and the beads can be seen at Arundel Castle today. The second rosary which Jane Kennedy was unable to rescue and which the Queen had worn was eventually burnt.

Of the many stories told of Mary Queen of Scots one is particularly apt. It appears that when she sailed from France to Scotland as a young woman, she brought with her the first sycamore trees to reach these islands, for there is a legend that as the Holy Family fled into Egypt, they rested beyond the city of Hermopolis in a grove of sycamores, and these trees have held people's imagination ever since.

Perhaps those devoted members of Mary Queen of Scot's household may have carved their prayer beads from these first sycamore trees. Because of its association with the Holy Land olive wood has always been considered suitable for rosaries, but beads can and have been made of anything from knots to rubies and there have been some strangely exotic materials used. St. Theresa of Avilla wore a rosary made from dried rose petals worked into the form of beads and as she walked along the cloisters of her Carmelite convent she was followed by the sweet scent of roses and this connection is sometimes claimed as the source of the word rosary. Appropriately, the Dominicans have in their care surely the strangest of all, for in the monastery of St. Sabina in Rome there is a rosary the beads of which are tiny dried and blackened oranges from a tree said to have been planted by St. Dominic for this monastery has been the headquarters of the Dominicans since 1222.

After the restoration when Catholics were free once more to practice their faith, the rosary quietly took its place in the overall liturgy of the Church, the days of childish care-free exhibitionism gone forever and a new maturity emerged in its stead. The days of the beadmakers of Paternoster Row and Ave Maria Lane are long gone, and the last bombing raid of Hitler's Luftwaffe in 1944 did extensive damage to the area although the street names survive.

Today prayer beads are mainly made of wood or glass and come from far and wide. There are only a few rosaries made in England. Most beads are made in Italy or in Ireland, and strange to discover, Communist Czechoslovakia is by far the biggest producer of beads in the world.

But the beads are only as important or valuable in the true sense as the prayers they count, for the rosary is there to lead men to think, to lift up their eyes to the hills, to Him "Who dwells in the heavens" and if there were no beads we could still do worse than imitate Robert Winchelsey, Archbishop of Canterbury in the fifteenth-century, who "no sooner was he free from business than he used at once, wherever he might be, to begin counting the Angelic Salutation on his fingers." (From Stephen Birchington in his *Life of Robert Winchelsey*).

CHAPTER FIVE

And the Pope has cast his arms abroad for agony and loss,
And called the kings of Christendom for swords about the Cross,
The cold queen of England is looking in the glass;
The shadow of the Valois is yawning at the Mass;
From evening isles fantastical rings faint the Spanish gun,
And the Lord upon the Golden Horn is laughing in the sun.

G. K. Chesterton "Lepanto".

THE BATTLE OF LEPANTO. Don Juan's flagship is in the middle distance, rather left of centre, with its standard of Christ crucified. — *Anonymous artist. Reproduced by permission of the Trustees of the National Maritime Museum, Greenwich, England.*

CHAPTER FIVE

WHILE the events of the Reformation continued their remorseless progress in Northern Europe, events in the south took place that were to ensure that the name of Lepanto would always be associated with Our Lady's prayer.

On the face of it, these events appear to contradict the peaceful role of the rosary, wresting it from gentle hands to be thrust into the rough calloused fists of war. It was at a time in history when Christian Europe stood in grave danger of being over-run and subjugated to the power of Islam and the dark foreboding cloud whose shadow had increased over the centuries now seemed to threaten Christians to the point where their days seemed numbered.

In practical terms Europe was in no state to withstand the concerted force that stood poised at its gate. That it did so was due in large measure to the power of the prayer of the rosary as the last knight of Europe came crusading across the seas with the fleets of Christian Europe in his wake. It was the last triumphant sea battle against Islam guided suitably enough by another Dominican Saint, Pope Pius V.

Far from the plains of Languedoc, across the Adriatic Sea where the fish curve and dive through emerald seas and the islands lie like jewels off the Peleponnese shores, there is even today in the air an unmistakable sensation of distant battle. In the sapphire spray there shimmers the image of galleys running before the wind, and the cries of Christian galley slaves beneath the blood-red crescent invade the air, mingling with jeers and laughter from beneath turbanned brows.

As the picture fades, the rattle of musket fire grows strong as the dipping oars touch the shore and yet in truth, it is only the sound of pebbles running before the ebbing tide.

For this is the bay of Lepanto lying beyond the Isthmus of Corinth where the greatest sea battle in history was fought on

October 7th, 1571. The events which led to this auspicious day had their beginnings far away on the plains of Arabia in the early part of the seventh-century when a young camel driver emerged from the desert to be acclaimed as the Prophet of Allah. From that day forth Islam was on the move.

By the end of the Prophet's life, by persuasion or the sword, all Arabs had been compelled to accept Islam, wave upon wave of Mogul warriors sprung from the Arabian plains to strengthen the arm of Mohammet's successors and the sword of the infidel carried the fight throughout the Eastern Mediterranean and into North Africa.

The full horror dawned painfully on the Christian world when in 638 Caliph Oman, Mohammet's conquering successor, rode into Jerusalem on a white camel and the holy lands were lost.

Spain succumbed to Islamic rule in 712 and the invading forces swiftly crossed the Pyrenees reaching as far north as Poitiers and as Gibbon observed: "a victorious line of march had been prolonged above a thousand miles of the rock of Gibraltar to the banks of the Loire; the repetition of an equal space would have carried the Saracens to the confines of Poland and the highlands of Scotland." Only the great victory of Charles Martel in 732 arrested their progress.

Gradually the Christian world raised itself, as if from a trance. The Crusades were marshalled by Pope Urban to recapture the Holy Lands and were undertaken by Christians from all parts of Europe. Their success was limited but the progress of Islam was temporarily halted and invasion of the west averted.

After a brief temporary respite, the Turkish Empire steadily increased in power and might until the sixteenth-century. On land their armies were made up of fighting men, or janissaries as they were known, whose success in battle was renowned for they placed no value whatsoever on their own lives, still less on others and obeyed orders instantly. In the Mediterranean the power of the Turks in the Islamic world had forged a cohesive and dauntingly invincible enemy, uniting squabbling factions under one sovereign, Suleyman the Magnificent of legendary and cynical cruelty.

There was just one minor irritation in an otherwise idyllic state of affairs for the Sultan. Since their expulsion from Rhodes by the Turks in 1565, the Knights of St. John had made their home on the Island of Malta. From there they ventured forth as corsairs constantly teasing and snapping at the tail of the huge dragon that was the Turkish fleet, as it plied to and fro on the direct route from its base in Constantinople to Tripoli in North Africa. Every relief ship sent by the Turks ran the risk of being intercepted and destroyed by the Knights and this was not to be tolerated by the man who considered himself the undisputed Emperor of East and West.

Forwarned by their agents in Constantinople of increased activity in the dockyards and arsenals, the Knights were prepared in some measure when the huge fleet of the Infidel sailed into sight, the personal standard of Suleyman the Magnificent glinting in the Mediterranean sun surmounting the largest and most beautiful ship that was ever seen on the Bosphorus. This was the flagship of Piali, Admiral of the Fleet under Mustapha Pasha, whose life long ambition it was to expel the Knights of Malta from the Mediterranean for once and for all.

Vastly outnumbered by the Turks, the Knights fought valiantly under their Grand Master, Jean de la Vallette in a seige that has become a legend of heroism. When the humiliated Turkish fleet finally withdrew in September they left fewer than 600 Knights alive on the Island while of 40,000 Turks, only 10,000 survived.

With hindsight it became clear that the Knights of Malta, who from their inception had pledged themselves to war against Islam, had by this victory taken the first step in the eventual defeat of that enemy. At the time, their triumph appeared heaven-sent in the eyes of those few battle worn survivors but to Christian Europe, which had watched with resigned pessimism from the outset and gradually with disbelief and elation, the outcome was nothing short of miraculous. To the Turk, it was a humiliating, and unforgiveable blow to the pride of Islam but by no means a mortal blow and the arsenal of Constantinople was seething with activity as the work of rebuilding the fleet began with heightened urgency. For retribution at its most terrible was the certain outcome of the crushing wound inflicted by the Knights of Malta on the all important prestige and pride of Suleyman the Magnificent.

The one man who saw quite clearly that an immense conflict of greater consequence than all that had gone before was imminent and that something extraordinary was needed if Europe was to be saved, was deep in prayer in the shadows of his private chapel in the Vatican.

The man who assumed the task of stemming the Islamic tide on the one hand, and of strengthening the nerve of the quaking Christian princes on the other, was not a bellicose statesman of great political prowess, but a monk of humble origin upon whom the mantle of the papacy fell. He was a Dominican thoroughly schooled in the disciplines of that order, and the task that faced him was in essence not unlike that which had faced St. Dominic. It was, after all, to protect the faith, the purpose for which the order had been founded; Pope Pius V was a worthy successor who fulfilled all the hopes of its founder. In the words of one commentator, he was one of those rare Christians who take all the words and examples of Christ literally, without exception or reservation, and so move through the world like a light in a dark place.

His government as Pope was firm as events demanded, for he was surrounded by vascillating rulers stumbling in confusion as they tried to balance compromise and concession. Despite his great age on becoming Pope, the Florentine Ambassador reported that he was "flourishing like a rose", and so diplomatic is the remark that one is left wondering whether or not the Pope was a thorn in his side. He was quite tireless in his efforts to rally the Christian princes and was driven to remark bitterly that they were responsible for the dire plight in which Europe found itself. For one who normally dwelt on loftier spiritual plains, he was practical enough to point bluntly to the fate that awaited all those defeated in battle by the Turks. For at a time when unity might have given a glimmer of hope to their cause, they were busily

occupied bickering amongst themselves. Both Germany and
France were making conciliatory noises to Constantinople, even
hoping for a share in the Islamic spoils in the seemingly inevitable
event of Turkish victory. England was out of the reckoning since
the Reformation which led eventually to the excommunication of
Elizabeth I, placing her firmly on the fence if not on the other side.

Chesterton in his epic poem on Lepanto expresses the plight of
the Pope most succinctly:

> And the Pope has cast his arms abroad for agony and loss,
> And called the kings of Christendom for swords about the Cross,
> The cold queen of England is looking in the glass;
> The shadow of the Valois is yawning at the Mass;
> From evening isles fantastical rings faint the Spanish gun,
> And the Lord upon the Golden Horn is laughing in the sun.

The only two nations remotely receptive to his plan to form a
Holy League against the Infidel were themselves deeply
suspicious of each other, for reasons it is interesting to explore.

The first of these was the state of Venice which lay at the other
end of the Mediterranean on the Adriatic Sea, her pink and white
palaces reflected in the blue lagoon that separates the Serenissima
from her immediate neighbours, her empire and government the
envy of the world. But behind the scenes, after nearly three hundred years of costly and largely ineffective defense against the
Turk, the courage of her rulers was at a low ebb. The Venetians
were not helped by their own strange inability to strike a balance
between spiritual matters and the more mundane subject of
political gain.

When Pope Urban urged the cause of the Crusades on them in
1203 they responded in a manner which illustrated only too vividly this conflict of interests which was to haunt them for centuries, for they never completed the arduous journey to the Holy
Land. Constantinople, the treasure house of the civilised world at
that time, lay in their path and proved too tempting to pass by.
All thoughts of crusading were banished as they fell upon the city
sacking and looting all before them, and with their galleons

almost sinking under the weight of priceless booty, they lumbered back to Venice. Perhaps the origin of the expression "turning a blind eye" comes from this enterprise, for their aged leader Dandolo was sightless and could justly claim to have seen nothing. This assault left Constantinople so weakened that when the Turks finally attacked in 1453 it fell with scarcely a struggle and the Turkish Empire, unwittingly aided by Venice, embarked upon a wave of expansion that was to last 200 years.

By the middle of the sixteenth-century, the threat to Venice itself was such that fear was no longer concealed behind gilded doors. In the last two hundred years they had witnessed the loss of all their possessions in the Aegean, and even their few outposts in the Adriatic coast were but pockets in occupied lands. The waters around the Peloponnese where centuries earlier the fleets of Anthony and Cleopatra had sailed, ceased to hold any charm for Venetian galleons. While at Navcos, inland from the bay of Lepanto, there lay the largest and southern most dockyard of the Islamic fleet.

While the Venetians spluttered with indignation, the evidence of their eyes did little to encourage them to take a bold stand or indeed a stand of any kind. Instead they drew up their chairs and proceeded to sign as many "peace" treaties as they could decently allow and as one Sultan succeeded another, the Venetians expressed the uneasy hope of renewed "relations". Unfortunately the "relations" envisaged by the Turk were of a different nature.

Having already crossed the Balkans and reached the gates of Vienna, the Turks were the undisputed masters of the Arab world and they saw little reason why their advance should stop short of Europe itself.

Mehmet II, the grandfather of Suleyman the Magnificent, had vowed that he would stable his horses beneath the Dome of St. Peter's and to wind the Pope's head in a turban. His grandson intended to fulfil his dream.

To the Venetians, already shocked into submission by all that had gone before, there came news in 1569 that an Islamic force

had landed on their treasured island of Cyprus. With uncustom-
ary bravado a fleet was dispatched, but it merely skulked around
the Mediterranean to return without honour, having failed to
engage the enemy once.

The Doges of Venice were better served by their military leader
in Famagusta, for he defended the beleaguered town for eleven
months against a force of 200,000 Turks. Bragadin had by his
side 8,000 Christians who eventually through exhaustion and
starvation were compelled to raise the white flag in surrender.
Duped by promises of free passage, they lay down their arms and
left the city, only to suffer instant death at the hands of the
Turks. A worse fate awaited their leader for he was taken to a col-
umn in the city square and, before the public gaze, slowly
skinned alive. The triumphant Turkish Admiral Mustaph sailed
away with the stuffed skin of Bragadin hanging from the yardarm
of his ship. It is hardly surprising that the Venetians were in an
outraged but receptive mood when Pope Pius appealed to them to
sign the League Treaty in 1570.

In Spain the situation could hardly have been more different. In
Philip II the country had a ruler of rare qualities, and yet he has
frequently been described as proud and devious for it has suited
some historians to see him through a glass very darkly indeed.

Proud he was, but not in the accepted sense of superiority or
personal haughtiness. He believed passionately in the Divine
Right of kings and was always deeply aware of the reverence due
to that station; he saw himself as the defender and champion of
Catholic Europe. When he was a child, his father Charles V, had
implanted in his conscience the importance of the monarchy in
protecting the people from the dangers that stalked the sixteenth-
century.

As if to underline the complex tasks that lay ahead and the
often incomprehensible contrariness of fate, he was born at the
moment when his father, the Holy Roman Emperor, and an in-
defatigable defender of the Catholic Church, was laying waste to
the Eternal City.

When only sixteen, due to his father's continual absence abroad, Philip was made Regent of Spain and on his father's abdication 1555, at the age of 29 he found himself King of one of the largest Empires the world had ever seen. King of Spain, of the Netherlands, of England (for he was by now married to Mary Tudor), master of Italy and Lord of such parts of the Western Hemisphere as had been explored, and of the Philippines so named in his honour, and above all, the right arm of the Church.

Even at that age, he so clearly perceived that Christ dwelt in the one holy Apostolic Church of Rome that he was prepared to stake treasures and kingdoms as well as his own peace of mind and health of body on that fact. This was the motive force which lay behind so many of the struggles in the Netherlands and France, and the reason why on numerous occasions when victory was his, he appeared to recoil from pressing the advantage or claiming valuable spoils, to the frustration of his generals and the profound disbelief of his opponents. For his quest was to free people to follow the faith and having achieved that objective, he returned home.

One of his council described him as "grave, serene and agreeable" and he was devoted to his family. There is a touching account of him reciting the rosary each day with his children when he was not on his travels, and on his death he bequeathed to his son a rosary of gold beads encrusted with nine rubies each, the cross with ten rubies.

His only failing was that perhaps sometimes he overestimated his personal importance in the eyes of God, for if he believed his cause to be just he was prepared to take arms against the Pope and indeed with a great sense of self-righteousness he once dispatched his own troops as his father had done before him, to march upon the Vatican. He frequently harboured a sense of injustice in the face of Papal disapproval for he felt, with some cause, that he drove himself to the point of bankruptcy in the defence of the Church.

It was on just such an occasion that the Pope turned to him with the request that he should once more muster his forces for the defence of Christendom.

The Turkish problem was nothing new to Spain. In the seventh-century the Muslims from North Africa had invaded Spain and only after the Crusades did the Spanish knights rise to reconquer their own lands finally succeeding during the reign of Philip's great grandparents, Isabel and Ferdinand.

However, in history nothing is ever so neatly cut and dried and the problem remained throughout successive centuries like an open and festering wound in the body of Spain. The indigenous population of Moriscos, as the Muslims became known, made their presence uncomfortably felt from time to time, and in 1558 the Turkish fleets sailed up and down the Italian coast inflicting unspeakable atrocities both there and on Sicily and Naples which were also Spanish possessions. Philip's fleet put to sea but beset by illness and finally panic on sighting the huge Turkish fleet, they were soundly defeated.

In spite of this reversal Philip was not entirely wholehearted in his response to the Papal request to form a Holy League against the Turk. His treasury was at an all time low, and this led the King to reply with a caution which was widely misunderstood. He felt bound to hedge his agreement with counter demands for financial help and concessions which appeared niggardly in the light of what was to follow and for one who could justly claim on his death bed to have spent a life in the service of the Church.

For the newly acceeded Sultan of the Turks, Selim the Sot, self-styled "Owner of all men's necks" it seemed that the time was ripe to fulfil his dream of snatching Europe. He was encourgaged by the knowledge that Philip was almost totally isolated amongst the Christian princes of Europe and not only did he have a rebellion on his hands in the south, but his armies were fully committed at the other end of Europe. The Sultan cherished the plan of turning the Mediterranean into a Turkish lake, from whence to proceed to Spain where his informers told him the Moriscos eagerly awaited his arrival.

Yet even as Philip pondered within the cold corridors of his unfinished palace of the Escorial, the Venetians courage was ebbing.

While arguing over the price of building ships, they were furtively considering a last minute deal with the Turks to avoid the awesome prospect of Ali Pasha at the head of his immense fleet.

None of these political conundrums and diplomatic manoeuvers were of the remotest interest to Pope Pius V. In long periods of silent prayer he contemplated only the principles behind all human behaviour, unclouded by triviality of any sort, and was able to see with complete clarity the situation as it really was. He was a true Dominican with the defence of the faith as his primary task amidst an awareness of the dangers which threatened to overwhelm Europe should it fall to Islam in the wake of North Africa and the Eastern Empire.

Beyond the conflicting political interests of Venice and Spain, Pius V had always represented the wider spiritual concept of a European alliance against the Turkish aggressions and he signed his name to the league agreement on March 7, 1571, the feast day of St. Dominic. With tears in his eyes he placed the Christian cause in the hands of Our Lady from whom the Spanish saint had received the rosary.

The devotion of Pius V to the Blessed Virgin had begun in childhood and her prayer of the rosary was specially dear to him, for the power of prayer over all human vanity was for this man proven beyond doubt. Only two years earlier in a Papal Bull he had instructed the faithful in the prayer of the rosary as the most powerful weapon against error. After he became Pope he was a familiar sight in the streets of Rome walking amongst the people clad still in the simple robes of a Dominican monk, deep in the prayer of the rosary and oblivious of all around him.

Despite all the political manoeuvering, he remained calmly aware of the real nature of the conflict and of the gravity of the threat which faced the Church. Of that he had no doubt. The only matter that ruffled the papal demeanour was the disarray amongst those who should have been unanimous in their support. The fact that his treasury reserves were at an all time low and in no state to finance the rebuilding of the Papal fleet was of secondary importance. His great generosity not only to the poor of Rome, but to the beleaguered English Catholics in exile and his endless ransom payments to the Turks for the release of Christian slaves, had almost emptied the Papal coffers.

Not the least achievement of this remarkable Pope was the welding together of two such disparate personalities, on the one hand the velvet piety of the Spanish and on the other the guilded duplicity of the Venetians, and yet these were united in the great fighting force that confronted Ali Pash on October 7, 1571. For if ever proof of the power of prayer was needed regardless of subsequent astonishing events, this surely was it. The sanctity of the Pope and his apparent aloofness from strife must have dumbfounded the practised diplomats of Madrid and Venice and after two months of haggling they duly signed the League Treaty.

Philip not only agreed to send his half-brother Don John of Austria to command the fleet but made a huge contribution in terms of ships and troops at a time when he was heavily committed elsewhere. In the event Spain undertook to provide half the total cost of the force with Venice supplying two-thirds of the remainder. The Pope and the Knights of Malta were left to find the final third. So amply were the prayers of the Pope answered that not only did the Venetians rebuild the small fleet of the Holy See, but in the battle that followed their Admiral placed himself and his fleets under the command of Don John, an undreamt of act of humility for a Venetian.

Amidst the melee of mounting excitement as preparations took place on both sides, there was only one figure who remained lost in silent thought. Selim the Sot, "Lord of all the Earth" gazing across the Adriatic, was heard to say softly that more than any galleys the Holy League could set against him, he feared the prayers of Pius V.

The power of the Papal prayer must have been renowned indeed for the Sultan uttered these words in the full knowledge that his own fleet was vastly superior to that of the Holy League. He could also take comfort in the knowledge that the legendary might of his fighting men was a daunting prospect for the strange and motley assortment that found themselves dispatched from different parts of Europe to sail under the banner of the Holy League. Even the Knights of Malta can have had little heart for renewed battle despite the rhetoric proclaiming the contrary which flowed from their drastically reduced numbers.

In July 1571 Don John finally set out from Madrid for Naples where he met Cardinal Granville to receive the banner of the Holy League and from there he proceeded to Messina to take command of the fleet that was assembling there. During those last weeks of July the allied squadrons gathered for their final councils of war and it was while the Venetian fleet was sailing to join them that the Sultan finally defeated the brave Bragadin in Cyprus.

Meanwhile when news that the grand fleet of the Turk had set sail from Constantinople reached Spain, Philip had travelled to the shrine of Our Lady of Guadalupe. All the events of the last few months culminated in this moment when the talking ceased and the reality of the battle ahead dawned on all those taking part.

To those who were apprehensive, the Pope commended the protection of Our Lady and the rosary was recited daily in every ship for the ensuing weeks. As the fleets gathered, Dominicans and Jesuits passed from deck to deck hearing confessions and offering Mass, while in Rome Pius V ordered prayers to be said in all convents and monasteries of the city. After days of prayer and fasting the fleet finally received orders to set sail.

The sight of the great armarda sailing from the harbour was an unforgetable one for the people of Messina to recount to their children and grandchildren. As each great galley jostled for position, the shouts of the galley masters and the cheers of the men mingled in the air with the cries of wheeling gulls and the screech of canvass unfurling in the azure sky. The noise almost drowned the murmur of prayer, as on every deck friars celebrated Mass, their vestments moving in the breeze.

As each ship reached the harbour mouth, the men knelt to receive the blessing of the scarlet clad Papal Nuncio. Don John, his golden armour gleaming in the Autumn sun, led the fleet from his flagship the Real, which sailed under the blue banner of Our Lady of Guadaloupe. As they rounded the corner and headed away from the mainland news reached them that the enemy had been sighted in the Gulf of Lepanto and they headed across the open sea to the straights of Ottranto.

Sailing down the Greek coastline, they saw signs of recent Turkish raids on the island of Corfu. The desecrated churches and the mutilated bodies of their victims bore witness to frenzied enemy attacks urging the Christian League to press on for they knew now that the enemy could not be far away.

On the evening of October 6th, Pius V led the prayer of the rosary at his own Dominican convent of Minerva in Rome, and on the morning of October 7, 1571 as the fog that had prevailed for several days dispersed, the fleet of the Holy League rounded the corner in full sight of the gulf of Lepanto and the enemy fleet.

In the moments that followed their arrival, the shouts and the clattering of swords and scimitars died away and there was an eerie silence as nearly 100,000 men prepared for battle.

Don John arranged his armada in three lines, the Venetians under their Admiral Venier on the left, The Genoese on the right and the young Admiral himself at the head of the Papal fleet in the center. The huge Turkish fleet sailed out of Navkapos Harbor in traditional Islamic crescent formation until on sighting the size of the Holy League force, they straightened into line abreast.

In the early morning light the crimson pennant emblazoned in gold with the words of the prophet billowed over the flagship Sultana, sailing under its anonymous Islamic Admiral Ali Pasha who carried as his macabre mascot the tooth of Mohammet encased in a crystal ball. In the last moments before battle commenced, Don John boarded the fastest of his brigantines and sailed along the lines of Christian ships inspecting his fleet and holding aloft a great iron cross. Returning to his flagship in silence, he unfurled a dazzling banner of blue damask with the figure of Christ crucified embroidered in gold thread surmounting the allied emblems.

The air was rent with tumultous cheering from every Christian ship almost drowning the shouting and jeering from the Turks, as the lines of galleys surged forwards.

The two flagships converged on each other at great speed and amidst the crashing and splintering of wood, they became locked in each others rigging thus creating a solid platform for the proceeding battle. For two hours wave upon wave of janissaries appeared from reserve ships to reinforce the hand to hand fighting.

Further to the left, the Turks tried to outflank the Venetian galleys by slipping through the narrows close to the coast, but this manoeuver was thwarted and the Venetians drove them aground.

Meanwhile the Knights of Malta came under heavy attack from the Turks with a score to settle after the Great Seige of Malta and the Knights fought with their customary courage but the numbers against them were overwhelming. In the melee, the Knights lost their flagship and with it the banner of St. John.

After sailing up and down the lines of his fleet, Don John placed himself in the vanguard where he could confront Ali Pasha in person. The Turkish Admiral was almost immediately felled by a cannon ball which instantly beheaded him. This was the turning point in the battle and by sunset the Turkish fleet was in total disarray.

The casualties were heavy; 7,500 Christian lives had been lost and twelve galleys sunk. Of the Turkish armada, all but forty-five of their ships had foundered, 30,000 men had perished and fifteen thousand Christian galley slaves were freed.

During the early evening on the day of the battle, Pope Pius V was in the midst of discussions in this small study in the Vatican when he suddenly broke away from his companions and crossed to the window.

He paused and with a radiant smile, turned to announce that a great victory had been won that day for the Holy League. This was more than two weeks before the official courier from Venice arrived in Rome. The victory of Lepanto exploded the myth of Turkish domination at sea, Ottoman sea power was contained for the foreseeable future in the Eastern Mediterranean and Europe breathed a sigh of relief.

In Rome, Pius V giving joyful thanks for the deliverance of Christian Europe, decreed that October 7th would thereafter be the feast of Our Lady of Victories.

For the Knights of Malta, the victory of Lepanto had an ironic significance. So complete was their triumph over Islamic sea power, that never again was there need for the monks of war to sail out beneath the Christian banner, and the Order gradually reverted to its original role of nursing.

The praises lavished on Don John by the allies and above all by the Pope were not wholeheartedly endorsed by Philip, who strangely denied his young Admiral a hero's welcome in Madrid. However, nothing can alter the fact that history acclaims this 24 year old Spanish prince for the execution of one of the finest victories at sea.

The pennant of the Turkish Admiral, Ali Pasha, was triumphantly carried to Spain where Philip caused it to be hung on the walls of the Escorial. Prayers of thanksgiving were offered throughout Spain, and Philip decreed that after his death his coffin should be lined with timbers from the Spanish galleons that had fought at Lepanto.

The Venetians were loud in their rejoicing and great was their pride when the galley Angelo Gabriele sailed into the lagoon trailing a Turkish flag and rows of turbans from its stern, and to this day the pennant holds pride of place on the ceiling of the Doges palace. Slightly faded over the years from its original scarlet, the golden inscription upon it is frayed from both the passage of time and the strains of battle.

The Venetians took great pride in the bravery of their sailors who had given their lives in greater numbers than any other ally, and their Admiral Sebastian Venier eventually succeeded as Doge of Venice.

In thanksgiving for such miraculous deliverance after three hundred years of continuous marauding by the Turkish fleet, the Venetians commissioned the building of a chapel to Our Lady of the Rosary. The walls were lined with records of the battle for there was no doubt in the Venetian mind of the cause of their victory and having proclaimed this debt, they inscribed the legend for all to see: *Non virtus, non arma, non duces sed Mariae Rosiae victores nos fecit* — neither valour, nor arms, nor leaders but Our Lady of the Rosary gave Victory.

Pius V lived just long enough to witness the great victory of Lepanto and died six months later. His successor Pope Gregory XIII in 1573 granted the Feast of Our Lady of Victories to all churches with an altar of the rosary and as if to prove the extreme caution of the Church in these matters, a century and a half passed before the feast was granted to the Universal Church.

With the Turkish threat at sea now a thing of the past it was nearly a century before the dread of Muslim invasion in Europe was banished. While the events of the Reformation continued to divide and occupy most of Europe, the Turks lost no opportunity to snap at the edges of the Empire until gradually the new found power of the Hapsburgs breathed life into the ailing alliance and the Christian forces gained the strength to gather themselves once more.

During a campaign that produced great deeds of courage in the face of vastly superior forces which was reminiscent of the seige of Malta so many years before, the beleaguered city of Vienna held out for six weeks in the summer of 1663. But the Turks had become sated with luxury and the picture they presented was quite different to the well ordered crescent of galleys that sailed into Christian view in 1571.

On this occasion they lumbered towards Vienna, a vast procession of 200,000 men led by Kara Mustapha whose Sultan vastly preferred hunting the forests of the Danube and whose 800 falcons wore collars and hoods encrusted with diamonds and pearls. But his Grand Vizier Mustapha was more business like and he settled his troops in 25,000 tents which formed a great circle around Vienna, and they prepared for a seige of limitless duration. However, not for the first time, and certainly not the last, the courage and faith of the Poles came to their rescue after a stirring and urgent appeal from Pope Innocent XI.

On September 3rd, the incarcerated citizens of Vienna saw flares in the sky which heralded their rescue, and under John Sobieska, the Polish horsemen came galloping down the hills to the north of the city, completely overpowering the Turkish army who were in rout by nightfall, leaving a strangely littered battlefield behind them.

The final victory over the Ottoman hordes came in 1716 when Prince Eugene defeated the remnants of the Islamic forces at Peterwarden, and it was then that Pope Clement XI commanded that the Feast of the Most Holy Rosary be celebrated by the Universal Church.

CHAPTER SIX

My sister, my bride is a garden enclosed,
the fountain sealed.

Song of Songs

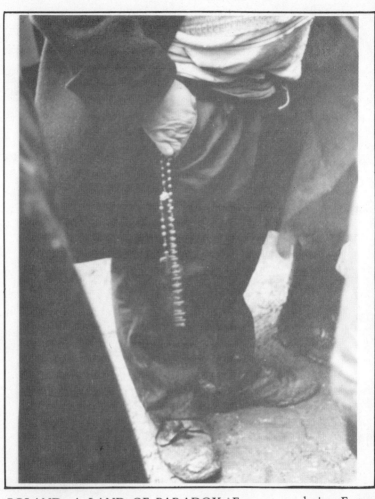

POLAND: A LAND OF PARADOX. Every year, during Easter week, a passion play is acted out on the wooded hills around Kalwaria Zebryzydowska, a small town in the rural area south east of Krakow. Thousands of Polish pilgrims gather at the monastery of the Bernardine monks which serves as a resting place and "home" for the pilgrims. These people follow the passion play as it takes the Way of the Cross, past seventeenth-century chapels over the rolling Beskid hills. This is a photograph of one of those pilgrims taken in 1988. — *Reproduced by kind permission of Janusz Rosikon.*

CHAPTER SIX

REVIEWING the events of 1572, Cardinal Newman wrote, "The battle of Lepanto arrested forever the danger of Mohammedan invasion in the south of Europe, and Lepanto was won by prayer".

After three hundred years of warfare, by prayer and great sacrifice, peace was once more restored in Southern Europe. In the north however the effects of the Reformation continued to be felt, and from the sixteenth-century Christian unity became a thing of the past. The religious wars that followed culminated in the French Revolution of the eighteenth-century.

The nineteenth-century saw the rise of Communism, the inevitable result of the turmoil of the previous centuries, and with it the appearance of Karl Marx, greeted by his followers as "the man who will drag down this God from His heaven".[1] And while the world was preoccupied with other matters, the remorseless march of totalitarianism that was to engulf so many nations in the twentieth-century was under way; there began the great struggle for the soul of modern man.

Europe that had once been the bastion of Christianity, had become weakened after the Renaissance when man began to tell God that he was no longer needed. Eventually it became a fertile breeding ground for Communism and Nazism, the horrors of the gas chamber and the concentration camp and all manner of cruelties and atrocities that paralise the imagination. Truth that is the right of every man, and freedom of spirit won for us at Calvary, became the hostage of totalitarianism and error.

In reality, Communism is a greater threat than Islam, for the Muslim acknowledges "Allah". It is interesting to note that when Spain was locked in civil war in 1936, the descendants of the Moors of Southern Spain came to the aid of the Catholics and gave their lives in great number to ensure a Christian victory, despite the considerable help given by the so called "Christian" countries to the Communists.

To the Communist there is no God, and therefore man has no special value. He is devoid of a soul, of any dignity, and certainly not entitled to the exercise of his God-given free will.

In the midst of this gathering gloom there appeared once more a light in the heavens. As the new Eve, so much loved and understood by the early Christians, Our Lady came to woo man back to Paradise by imploring him to return to her Son, and with increasingly dire warnings if her message was to be ignored.

In 1830 Our Lady appeared to St. Catherine Laboure in the rue du Bac, Paris and again in France in 1846 to two small children at La Salette. On each occasion Our Lady spoke of the anger of her Son, and the need for prayer and penance. As her message remained unheeded, so the apparitions became more frequent and more insistant.

In Lourdes in 1858, a lonely child unable to cross the river to play with her friends, wandered up the bank to Massabielle. There the beautiful "lady" appeared to her and prayed the rosary with her. In words that Bernadette did not understand, but repeated faithfully to the parish priest, the lady told her, "I am the Immaculate Conception".

The many cures that have taken place in Lourdes since 1860 bear witness to the authenticity of the apparitions and remove all reasonable doubt. The message as always was for prayer and penance.

There was a gap of twelve years between the apparitions at La Salette and Lourdes. Men began to listen and as Our Lady had requested, chapels were built and pilgrims came in their thousands. But still the message had not sufficiently been grasped, and a terrible war was to overtake the world before Our Lady appeared once more.

This time the mountains of Portugal were chosen, the land which forms part of the Iberian Peninsula with Spain, the birthplace of St. Dominic and the land from which Don John of Austria sailed forth to Lepanto.

The timing of this apparition was crucial. While the world still reeled from the onslaught of war, an event of even more ominous importance was taking place in Russia. In 1917, in St. Petersburg now Leningrad, atheistic Communism was launched on the world and twenty seven days after the outbreak of that revolution, Our Lady appeared in Fatima and laid down the only conditions for peace in the world, and for staving off the punishment of God.[2] This time, when asked by the three small children who she was, Our Lady replied "I am the Lady of the Rosary", and once more instructed them to follow her in prayer. Francis, who alone of the three was unable to see her, was told to take up his beads and pray. As soon as he did so his eyes were opened and he too could see the "beautiful lady".

Our Lady requested the children to return on the 13th of each month, and on July 13, 1917, spoke these words: "I shall ask for the consecration of Russia to my Immaculate Heart, as well as communion of reparation on the first Saturday of the month. If my requests are granted Russia will be converted and there will be peace. Otherwise Russia will spread her errors through the world, raising up wars and persecutions against the Church. Many will be martyred, the Holy Father will have much to suffer, several nations will be wiped out. The outlook is therefore gloomy. But my Immaculate Heart will finally triumph; the Holy Father will consecrate Russia to me; she will be converted and an era of peace will be conceded to the world. In Portugal the faith will always be preserved.

At the close of the Holy Year in 1951, solemn High Mass was sung in Fatima in the Russian Uniate Rite, by a bishop who had recently escaped from a Soviet prison. "Russia will be converted" Our Lady said, and in Fatima the Icon of Our Lady of Kazan is kept in safe keeping until such time as it is returned to its home in Russia.

But it is as if a struggle of titanic proportions is being enacted. In contrast to the growing awareness of the message of Fatima, there is an unprecedented spread of evil in the world. Wars break out in the four corners of the globe and there are lunatic and frenzied acts of terrorism that inflict untold suffering on the innocent. Many have experienced the breakdown of family life, the divorce rate soars, the abortion figures are rocketing and it seems as if in the midst of this shambles the world is bent on self destruction.

Always when events appear to be hurtling out of control and the odds insuperable, Our Lady chooses to come to our assistance. Like any mother who sees her children stray closer and closer to danger, she calls us to safety and begs us repeatedly to return to her Son. We know that she is right and we know that the prayer of the rosary works, so totally compelling is its history.

How hopeless the situation must have seemed to St. Dominic; how overwhelming the task that confronted St. Pius V as the mantle of Islam seemed to be on the brink of engulfing the entire Christian world. In worldly terms both situations had all the ingredients of lost causes.

Peace is a word much bandied about today, and sometimes almost with an air of aggression, the word is chanted by the least peaceful of crowds. The ageless longing for peace is no nearer fulfilment, in fact the reverse seems to be true.

When the angel appeared to the shepherds at Bethlehem, he too used the word peace, but added that vital proviso which is often forgotten or ignored, "to men of good will".

The Albigenses, the Turks or the Communists, who can stop such apparently overwhelming forces, but the grace of God? Certainly men are ill equipped to face such insuperable odds. But for "men of good will" armed with the grace of God, there is no limit to what they can achieve.

Sometimes in the rush of our own lives, our problems seem large enough without worrying about larger issues, and in any case what can we do?

It is interesting that Our Lady did not appear to those in power, to politicians or leaders of this world. It might have avoided all the confusion and disbelief encountered by those who were given such world shattering messages had she done so.

In most instances the children did not even understand the message themselves and had to repeat the Lady's words, in order carefully to relay them later and then to face the inevitable scepticism that followed.

Our Lady was not drawn to the worldly or sophisticated of this world, but to innocence. They were not even particularly saintly; the children at Fatima obediently said their prayers, but would rush through them only saying the first words of each prayer so that they could return to their games, but in their innocence they knew no better. Like the apostles chosen before them, their hearts were full of love.

Our Lady is not unreasonable in her demands, she knows that not all men will embrace her message, and asks only that enough people will recite her prayer, and we who always seek proof know her words to be true.

When the Soviets left Vienna in 1955 their withdrawal was complete and with hindsight to many, inexplicable, for it was the only withdrawal from foreign territory since their period of expansion began in 1917. However, it is on record that some 700,000 people were committed to the Confraternity of the Rosary and their prayers were answered. The date of the Soviet withdrawal was the 13th of May, the anniversary of Fatima.

How different were the children after seeing the "beautiful Lady". Their only wish was to be with her, to pray as she had commanded and to grieve over the sins of the world which so offend our Lord. "Men must amend their lives and ask pardon for their sins. Men must no longer offend Our Lord, who is already offended too much". These words were spoken at Fatima on the day of the great miracle of the sun, a miracle promised by Our Lady to the children who repeatedly asked her for a sign to those who doubted.

The miracle has been well documented both by press reports and accounts given by many of the thousands who witnessed the sun apparently tumbling from the sky, before spinning and casting strange beams of light across the earth. Many who came, out of curiosity and scepticism, like the director of the Lisbon daily paper, *O Seculo*.

However, his report of October 15th ends with the words: "Only one thing remains now to be done, namely for the scientists to explain from the height of their learning the fantastic dance of the sun, which today at Fatima, has drawn "Hosanna" from the hearts of the faithful; and which, as trustworthy people assure me, has impressed even Free-thinkers, as well as others of no religious convictions, who had come to this spot, henceforth celebrated."

Celebrated it most certainly is, with an immense Basilica built near the spot at the Cova da Iria where Our Lady appeared, now constantly thronging with thousands of pilgrims who travel from all over the world, many of whom complete the last two hundred miles on foot. Throughout the day and night the prayer of the rosary is recited in every language. And two miles beyond the Basilica, visits are made to the little village of Ajustral where the children lived.

The cobbled path which is still the country route to Ajustral winds its way through the groves of olive and pine trees and the wild thyme that grows amongst the rocks; past the Stations of the Cross, each one donated by a different Hungarian parish whose members, expelled by Communism, are now scattered throughout the United States. The path continues to the 14th Station at the top of the hill, where there is a chapel dedicated to St. Stephen, King of Hungary.

From there, one gazes from the little village of Fatima on one side to the extraordinary testimony of the twentieth-century to the miracle of the Cova da Iria, now a mass of hotels and mother-houses of religious orders from around the world, and towering over all, the slender spire of the Basilica topped by a golden crown, its bells pealing out the song of Fatima on the hour.

The sounds amongst the olive groves are probably no different now than they were sixty years ago, the song of birds, the distant bleating of goat herds, dogs barking and from Ajustral, the harsh voices of women as they work in the fields. The only alien sound is the hammering of builders as more and more accommodations for the millions of pilgrims are built.

Amidst this scene one comes upon the spot where Our Lady appeared to the three children on the one occasion when they were prevented from keeping their appointment at the Cova da Iria, the same trees moving gently in the breeze, and all stray thoughts fade from the mind. Peace and silence invade the air and one is lost in gratitude.

Who can forget the first time they saw the grotto at Lourdes? These events are deeply moving, never to be forgotten.

How easy it is in the euphoria of a pilgrimage to overlook the dire message of Our Lady, and to return home in a glow of piety, quite forgetting that we are commanded to change our lives, to convert ourselves before we can hope to convert others.

For it is certain that our enemies will not be struck by lightning, that is not God's way. When we have fulfilled Our Lady's wishes there will be peace. That is the great message of Fatima: "My Immaculate Heart will finally triumph; the Holy Father will consecrate Russia to me. She will be converted and an era of peace will be conceded to the world". Because she is a mother, Our Lady knows how easily distracted we can be, and so not only do we have her words to ponder but clues are laid across the trail to capture our attention.

There can be no life without water, and at La Salette, Lourdes and Fatima, water sprang from the barren ground at Our Lady's command, to heal both body and spirit. "My sister, my spouse is like a garden enclosed, a fountain sealed."

The "garden enclosed" was the mediaeval symbol of the Incarnation, the Incarnation upon which Christianity is based, that gives so true an understanding of the world, the marriage of matter and spirit, the divine and the human, for whom the prayer of the rosary, involving both mind and body, is so perfectly suited.

The "garden enclosed", beloved of the early Christian, was represented by a chaplet of roses that became the circlet of beads to be carried through the centuries, to the centuries of Lourdes and Fatima, to encircle a world torn apart and to heal with prayer the wounds of Christ's Body on earth. We know that it will be so; we have the promise of the Mother of God.

The Mysteries
of the Rosary

THE JOYFUL MYSTERIES

1. *The Annunciation*

And in the sixth month the angel Gabriel was sent from God into a city of Galilee called Nazareth: To a virgin espoused to a man whose name was Joseph, of the house of David; and the virgin's name was Mary. And the angel, being come in, said unto her: Hail, full of grace, the Lord is with thee; blessed art thou among women. Who, having heard, was troubled at his saying and thought with herself what manner of salutation this should be. And the angel said to her: Fear not, Mary, for thou has found grace with God. Behold, thou shalt conceive in thy womb and shalt bring forth a son; and thou shalt call his name Jesus. He shall be great and shall be called the Son of the Most High. And the Lord God shall give unto him the throne of David His father; and He shall reign in the house of Jacob for ever. And of His kingdom there shall be no end. And Mary said to the angel: How shall this be, because I know not man? And the angel answering, said to her: The Holy Ghost shall come upon thee and the power of the Most High shall overshadow thee. And therefore also the Holy One which shall be born of thee shall be called the Son of God. And, behold, thy cousin Elizabeth, she also hath conceived a son in her old age; and this is the sixth month with her that is called barren. Because no word shall be impossible with God. And Mary said: Behold the handmaid of the Lord; be it done to me according to thy word. And the angel departed from her. (LUKE 1:26-38)

Mary was a young girl of thirteen or fourteen when this event took place. As far as we know, she had been brought up by her loving parents St. Anne and St. Joachim, under the law of the Jewish faith. We know from the words of the angel that she was "full of grace" and no more wonderful description could be given. For it tells us that she was without sin, a creature so pleasing to God, that as He intended for us all, her soul was literally a reflection of Divine Love.

With her humility came also great prudence, for Our Lady was "troubled at his saying and thought with herself what manner of salutation this should be". Mary was calmed by the words of the angel "fear not" and that in itself is astonishing for in the sheltered and peaceful tenor of her life, such a cosmic occurance would be enough to unnerve the sturdiest heart, and the words of the angel which followed were no less alarming. For what followed was the announcement of the most important event in the history of the world since the banishment from Paradise. The future of the human race hung in balance for one tantalising moment while heaven and earth were held in suspense awaiting the *fiat* or acceptance of Our Lady.

The prudence of Our Lady, her humility and trust in God, merely prompted her to enquire of the angel the manner in which this event could take place, "since I know not man". One can only speculate on the consequences of the angel's demand. Our Lady was betrothed to St. Joseph but not yet married. In the law of the time it was not unknown for a child to be born to a betrothed couple, and such a child was considered legitimite. If, however, the woman had been unfaithful to her betrothed, death by stoning was the usual punishment. Joseph knew all this to be unthinkable, but one can imagine the depth of inward crisis this holy man must have undergone.

This was not the only concern, for like all brought up in the Jewish faith, Our Lady's knowledge of the scriptures was extensive and she must therefore have been aware of the terrible fate that awaited the Son of God, and the suffering that was entailed in her acceptance.

None of these speculations appears to have clouded her submission and acceptance of the will of God. And having received Our Lady's words "Be it done unto me according to thy word", the angel left her without further ado, without any consoling explanation or comfort, and the future of the human race was ensured.

2. *The Visitation*

And Mary, rising up in those days went into the hill country with haste into the city of Juda. And she entered into the house of Zachary and saluted Elizabeth. And it came to pass that, when Elizabeth heard the salutaion of Mary, the infant leaped in her womb; and Elizabeth was filled with the Holy Ghost. And she cried out with a loud voice and said: Blessed art thou among women and blessed is the fruit of thy womb. And whence is this to me that the mother of my Lord should come to me? For behold, as soon as the voice of thy salutation sounded in my ears, the infant in my womb leaped for joy. And blessed art thou that hast believed because these things shall be accomplished that were spoken to thee by the Lord. (LUKE 1:39-45)

The journey that Mary embarked upon was daunting. In a land that was rife with violence, she undertook the journey on foot, accompanied, tradition relates, by one female attendant. It is a lesson to us that having accepted the will of God, Our Lady did not just sit back and await events. But, knowing that her cousin was in need of her, without hesitation, she set off at once to be with Elizabeth.

The joy of heaven in that new life (in human terms) enfolded within the womb of Our Lady is echoed in the words of the Song of Songs:

For winter is now past, the rain is over and gone. The flowers have appeared in our land: the time of pruning is come; the voice of the turtle is heard in our land: the fig-tree hath put forth her green figs; the vines in flower yield their sweet smell. Arise, my love, my beautiful one, and come.

And Our Lady brought that Child within her to Elizabeth as she brings Him to us if we will only turn to her. She need not have feared for Elizabeth's understanding, for, inspired by the Holy Spirit, her cousin greets her with the words of the angel Gabriel, "Blessed art thou amongst women. . . ." And the unborn St. John leaps in greeting of his Lord.

The words of the Magnificat uttered in reply to Elizabeth remind us once more of the remarkable knowledge which Our Lady appears to have had of the Old Testament, for there is not one line which is not full of allusion to the Bible in this joyful announcement that God has visited his people.

This is the longest utterance recorded of Our Lady, who is normally so sparing of words. It is interesting that on this occasion Our Lady's humility took on a different guise. She was so overwhelmed with joy that she became transported with happiness.

My soul doth magnify the Lord
And my spirit hath rejoiced in God my Saviour,
Because he hath regarded the humility of his handmaid;
For behold from henceforth all generations shall call me blessed
Because He that is mighty hath done great things to me;
    and holy is His name.
And His mercy is from generation unto generation,
    to them that fear Him.
He hath shewed might in His arm; He hath scattered the proud
    in the conceit of their heart.
He hath put down the mighty from their seat and hath
    exalted the humble.
He hath filled the hungry with good things; and the rich
    he hath sent away empty.
He hath received Israel his servant, being mindful of his mercy
As He spoke to our fathers; to Abraham and to his seed for ever.

(LUKE 1:46-55)

There is limitless meditation in those lines; from them we learn the answer to so many problems which beset us in this life.

3. The Nativity

And it came to pass that when they were there her days were accomplished that she should be delivered. And she brought forth her first-born son and wrapped him in swaddling clothes and laid him in a manger because there was no room for them in the inn. And there were in the same country shepherds watching and keeping the night-watches over their flock. And behold, an angel of the Lord stood by them and the brightness of God shone round about them; and they feared with a great fear. And the angel said to them: Fear not; for, behold, I bring you good tidings of great joy that shall be to all the people; For this day is born to you a Saviour, who is Christ the Lord, in the city of David. And this shall be a sign unto you: You shall find the infant wrapped in swaddling clothes and laid in a manger. And suddenly there was with the angel a multitude of the heavenly army, praising God and saying: Glory to God in the highest; and on earth peace to men of good will. (LUKE 2:6-14)

Caesar Augustus was intent on the grandiose plan of taking a census of the world. Since, as far as the planners of the time were concerned, the world meant the Roman Empire, notices went up everywhere ordering people to return to their town of origin to register. Despite the imminence of the birth of the Holy Child, there must have been some urgency about the matter, for St. Joseph felt impelled to set out immediately on the five mile journey from Jerusalem to Nazareth.

Poor St. Joseph must have felt confident of finding shelter somewhere in his home town, despite the thronging crowd arriving from all directions to obey Caesar's command. As they went from door to door, becoming increasingly tired, it became apparent that whereas the Roman soldiers and other wealthy visitors had found shelter, for them there was nothing, and that sad line "There was no room at the inn" echoes forlornly in St. Luke's Gospel. There was no room for the Creator in His Creation. Eventually room was found in a stable beneath the inn, used normally by the shepherds. True holiness is so often where one least expects to find it, and there Our Lady brought forth her Child.

It is apt that the animals should be present at the birth of God made man, untrammelled by human considerations, they stayed quietly by the manger, unaware of the astounding event taking place in their midst, but sleeping peacefully in the presence of their Maker.

Our Lord did not announce Himself to all the world, but through an angel to some shepherds, and by a star to the wise men. Two completely different sorts of people; the shepherds who in their simplicity recognised Divinity and the Magi who in their wisdom were not influenced by appearances.

To the shepherds who came immediately, the poverty was not strange; they knew that King David was himself a shepherd, and the words of the angel filled them with joy. The Magi were slightly more cautious as the clever have a tendency to be, and took the precaution of verifying the direction of the star with the court of King Herod, a fatal diversion. How fast the news must have travelled for the priests and scribes were able to tell them immediately which direction to take.

To Herod the news was grim indeed. He knew the prophecies foretold the end of his rule with the coming of the Messiah, and he sought to forestall the will of God by striking out violently against the innocent, the reaction of tyrants throughout history.

How we wince in pity at the massacre of the innocents, and yet that crime is continued to this day in the abortion clinics around the world. We must pray that the world will recognise the sanctity of life, the rights of children and the duty we have to protect and care for each new life for it is indeed a gift from God.

Apart from theological matters, what individual qualities mark those who have lived after the Nativity at Bethlehem from those who have lived before?

The old Roman meaning of charity was love of family or close relations, an interested love. After Bethlehem, charity was transformed by the love of that small Baby for the entire human race. We see the fruits today when people separated by thousands of miles can be moved to loving pity and aid for others who are starving; in the work of Mother Theresa for the poor, and in the hospices throughout the world who care lovingly for the dying. All this disinterested love flows from the stable at Bethlehem.

Humility, too, has taken on a new meaning from the old interpretation of lowness or meanness. No longer the false modesty dictated by good manners which makes people deny gifts given them by God, nor the obsequiousness of fawning to superiors, but the humility of the man who silently and happily places others before himself, who accepts injustice without rancour; that is the humility that comes from Bethlehem where the Son of God was born in a stable.

4. *The Presentation in the Temple*

And after the days of her purification, according to the law of Moses, were accomplished, they carried him to Jerusalem, to present him to the Lord. Every male opening the womb shall be called holy to the Lord; And to offer a sacrifice. . . . (LUKE 2:22-24)

As it is written in the law of the Lord, a pair of turtledoves or two young pigeons.

Under the law of Moses, a mother was considered unclean after the birth of a child, and had to present herself at the temple to be purified, at the same time presenting her first born son. Despite the fact that Mary was the mother of God, there was no exemption for her, neither did she in her humility ever seek to do other than follow the law in obedience.

Normally the offering was a lamb, but owing to their extreme poverty Our Lady and St. Joseph were permitted to offer two turtledoves. We are told of that holy pair, Simeon and Anna who were present in the Temple. Simeon had waited and prayed throughout his long life in the Temple and immediately recognized in the Holy Child, the Redeemer he had awaited for so many years. Inspired by the Holy Spirit he uttered the beautiful words of the *Nunc dimittis*:

Now thou dost dismiss thy servant, O Lord, according to
Thy word in peace;
Because my eyes have seen thy salvation
Which thou hast prepared before the face of all peoples;
A light to the revelation of the Gentiles and the glory of thy
people Israel. (LUKE 2:29-32)

How patiently he had waited, and how wonderfully that patience was rewarded. Anna too had waited many lonely years for that same joy, probably one of those faithful women one sees busying themselves around churches everywhere, but Our Lord knew that her heart was true, and her patience was also rewarded.

As for Our Lady, she was told that a sword of sorrow would pierce her heart, but she must have already feared that. What pathetic fears we have for ourselves and seek to overcome that fear with idle reassurance. We are protected from knowledge of the future, but for Our Lady her suffering was spelled out unmercifully while she held the Baby in her arms.

5. *The Finding in the Temple*

And, when he was twelve years old, they going up to Jerusalem, according to the custom of the feast, and having fulfilled the days, when they returned, the child Jesus remained in Jerusalem. And his parents knew it not. And thinking that he was in the company they came a day's journey and sought him among their kinsfolks and acquaintances. And, not finding him, they returned into Jerusalem, seeking him. And it came to pass that, after three days, they found him in the temple, sitting in the midst of the doctors, hearing them and asking them questions. And all that heard him were astonished at his wisdom and his answers. And, seeing him, they wondered. And his mother said to him: Son, why has thou done so to us? And he said to them: How is it that you sought me? Did you not know that I must be about my Father's business? And they understood not the word that he spoke unto them. (LUKE 2:42-50)

The Holy Family responds once more to the dictates of the law which requires that all men should attend the three great feasts of the Passover, Pentecost and the Tabernacles. On reaching the age of twelve, Jesus was considered mature in the eyes of that law, and therefore was able to join his parents for the first time.

The loss of Our Lord for three days is one of the Seven Sorrows of Our Lady. Not only did she suffer as any mother who looses a child, but in her heart she knew that her Son would be put to death by His own people. Since Jesus had now reached maturity she must have wondered if the time of His death was upon them. Mary suffered the dark night of all who lose God, and she would suffer again for the three days between the Crucifixion and the Resurrection.

Aelred, Abbot of Rievaux, pointed out in a sermon on the Finding in the Temple that Our Lord often withdraws Himself for a short time, in order to make us search more carefully for Him, and that this mystery is the emblem of the devout soul.

Jesus is always to be found in unexpected places. How amazed, apart from being relieved, must Mary and Joseph have been to find Jesus in the school of Rabbis, seated amongst the pupils before the learned priests and scribes. What a wonderful sight that conjures in the mind, the Child of twelve sitting calmly before the elders, their minds befuddled with layers of legislative knowledge and yet they listen attentively to the wisdom of their Lord and God. St. Luke, with great economy of words, says simply that they were "astonished".

The last words on the subject from St. Luke do not end there, for he adds: "And he went down with them and came to Nazareth and was subject to them. And his mother kept all these words in her heart. And Jesus advanced in wisdom and age and grace with God and men."

The contrast between the words of Jesus to His mother in the temple in which He teaches us that the things of God must come before all that we love most in this world and the wonderful image of life within the Holy Family evoked by St. Luke are the reason for this mystery being firmly placed amongst the joys.

THE SORROWFUL MYSTERIES

1. *The Agony in the Garden*

When Jesus had said these things, he went forth with his disciples over the brook Cedron where there was a garden, into which he entered with his disciples. (JOHN 18:1)

Once more we hear of a garden, at another crucial moment in the events that led to our redemption. As the banishment of the human race took place in a garden, so to a garden Our Lord now returned.

Fra Angelico portrays the Garden of Gethsemene as a place of great beauty, full of olive and lemon trees, with carpets of jewel-like flowers. For him Paradise is never far away, and above all it is here as the drama unroles. Our Lord is seen in the distance kneeling in the gently folding hills of Mount Olive with an angel hovering nearby to give comfort. And in the foreground, bathed in moonlight, are the carefully arranged figures of Peter, James and John; a peaceful and tender scene.

How different the reality must have been, as Our Lord went up to the rocky path to kneel in prayer, with the sharp stones cutting into His knees. As if to underline the rocky nature of the countryside, St. Luke describes Our Lord withdrawing from the others a "stone's cast". Rather than the soft caressing moonlight suggested by Fra Angelico, the rocks must have cast foreboding shadows across the hill, the twisted limbs of olive trees standing eerily on the skyline like some distended cross, announcing the gathering forces of evil to an already bleak scene.

The sounds in the distance of the gathering mob, the shouts and crack of sticks being torn from the ground to enforce rage, all carried on the still night air to the place where Jesus knelt.

Even in His hour of desolation, Jesus still teaches us with loving awareness of our weakness. To what immense lengths we will go to avoid suffering; whole industries are involved in producing

132

panaceas for all ills, to such an extent that the belief is firmly held that to suffer at all is a grievous injustice and it is the right of every person to be free from all discomfort. To the saints suffering became the very means of salvation. Our Lord prayed until His sweat turned to drops of blood, for through His Divinity Christ knew precisely what was to befall Him during the hours of excruciating torture that lay ahead, and even more serious was the knowledge of the sin that would continue to be committed and unrepented until the end of time. He prayed: "My Father, if this chalice may not pass away but I must drink it, thy will be done." (MT. 26-42). We are told of the angel who was sent to comfort Him.

There is another lesson to be pondered over from this desolate scene. Our Lord turned for comfort to the three disciples, St. Peter the rock on which he founded His Church, St. John the Beloved, and his brother James, and they responded by falling asleep. The New Testament has several warnings to us to remain spiritually alert; and above all the words of Jesus to the three disciples: "Watch ye; and pray that you enter not into temptation. The spirit indeed is willing, but the flesh is weak." (MARK 14-38).

But eventually their drowsy watch was brought to an abrupt halt as the din of the approaching mob grew louder, and they went forward to meet the crowd.

2. *The Scourging at the Pillar*

At the end of the long night of agony, there came what St. Matthew describes as a great multitude with swords and clubs. St. John is more graphic and tells of the mob which "cometh thither with lanterns and torches and weapons."

Human nature is consistent in this one respect, for have not the mob always been enraged beyond reason by the innocent. We see them in practically every newspaper we pick up, angry faces with clenched fists and twisted jeering faces. Always a crowd, for the bully is a coward and needs others to aid and abet his cruelty to the weak. Each time that mob marches in hatred Christ is scourged again.

And along they all came, egging each other on with shouts and waving arms until anti-climatically coming to a clattering halt in front of Jesus. Lost for the moment, they seem unable to decide on their next move, standing there rather stupidly, and St. John tells us that Judas stood with them. And when Jesus quietly enquires of this sea of faces "Whom seek ye?" and replies to their demand, "I am He", they stumble back, falling over each other.

For one precious second the Voice of Innocence silences evil, but the betrayal of Judas ensures that the crowd, now even more enraged by shame, grasps Jesus and to justify their fury, they bind His hands with rope. Such is the power of innocence that this huge mob felt safe only when Our Lord, alone and defenceless, was tightly bound. For we know the blunt truth that by now the disciples had abandoned Jesus and run away into the night.

St. John tells us that Jesus was first led to Annas, before going on to Caiphas, his son-in-law and High Priest, and there the priests, elders and scribes looked for some means of condemning Him.

There was no shortage, as there never is, of people rushing forward to invent accusations, but even in these extraordinary circumstances, the evidence was ludicrous. Eventually the High Priest rose to his feet, subduing the rabble to ask if He was indeed "the Christ, the Son of God", to which Jesus replied, "Thou has said it". Triumphant that he might at last have a case the Chief Priest turns, like any tyrant, to his cowed followers for approval. But another problem now looms for the mob, their law forbade them to put a man to death, they could go no further therefore than replying that He was "guilty of death". Someone else must be found to carry out that sentence, and they knew that Pontius Pilate was their man.

Some earlier misdemeanour had resulted in relative banishment to this outpost of the Empire for the uneasy Pilate. Relations with Rome were further soured when he attempted to erect images of the Emperor and himself in the Temple, and the local Jews whose support he badly needed to retain any credibility as Governor before Rome were enraged by his actions. Even so, Pilate could so easily have become St. Pilate if he had found the courage to follow his conscience, for from the outset he was aware of the innocence of the prisoner thrust before him.

He is mystified at first by the babbling of vague accusations, "we have found this man perverting our nation, and forbidding to give tribute to Caesar"; in St. John's account, they appear even more shifty, unable to find anything more convincing than "if he were not a malefactor, we would not have delivered him up to you", but now comes the real reason for their envy and hatred and Pilate recognizes it immediately, "And saying that he is Christ the King".

Pilate now understands the situation, as far as he is able, and knows what the mob requires of him. He is in an agony of indecision, and all the while the crowd never ceases its clamouring and shouting. When he hears the words of Jesus, "Everyone that is of the truth heareth my word" Pilate replies wearily, "What is truth", and he returns to the Jews saying, "I find no cause in Him". He offers to release one prisoner to them as was the custom on the feast. His offer is drowned in a deafening roar of "crucify Him", and Pilate capitulates to the rule of the mob. How blind we are in our efforts to save our skin in the eyes of the world; Pilate had one last desperate card to play.

In sending Our Lord to be scourged, he clung to the hope that the bloodlust of the crowd might be satisfied and shamed into releasing Him. This was the greatest cruelty. Scourging was often inflicted on the condemned before crucifixion for it produced a fever and ensured that the pains of death would be exacerbated and prolonged. It was inflicted by several soldiers with metal tipped leather thongs, and was continued until a state of excruciating physical agony was achieved, but stopped short of death so as to ensure that the victim could suffer death on the Cross.

3. *The Crowning with Thorns*

And they clothed him with purple; and, platting a crown of thorns, they put it upon him. And they began to salute him; Hail, King of the Jews. And they struck his head with a reed; and they did spit on him. And bowing their knees, they adored him. (MARK 15:17-19).

Here, if ever it was needed, is the evidence that things are rarely as they appear. This sad and bleeding figure is the Saviour of the world. Think how earthly kings and leaders are surrounded by pomp and circumstance, and today, by layers of security, and yet this pathetic figure was the Son of God, the King of all Kings, the Creator of the world that now mocked and spat upon Him. The sin of mankind gave vent to terrible vengeance as He freely took upon Himself torture and death for our sin, and His love for His creation is indeed beyond all human comprehension.

The irony of the situation was intended. The real reason for the hatred and determination of the Chief Priests and the Pharisees was Our Lord's claim to be the King of the Jews. Such an event had been foretold in the prophecies, which they well knew, and now to their horror looked like being fulfilled; their rule would be at an end if such were the case. For the soldiers, who had so cruelly beaten the prisoner, no such biblical predictions clouded their minds. They merely looked upon such claimants, and there were several, as tiresome troublemakers causing civil disturbances and putting more work on the military.

And now, with all the energy of bullies let loose on the innocent, they set about Jesus, crushing a circlet of thorns into His forehead. Seeing Him seated, the blood pouring down His face onto the cloak, already clinging to open wounds, their sarcasm knew no bounds. They knelt before Him, sneering in mock obeisance. Having handed him the sceptre of weakness, a reed, they snatched it from Him to hammer the thorns more deeply into His brow.

And then it appears that Pilate, the man, moves away from Pilate the Governor, and is alone before his Creator. He asks in almost childlike curiosity where He comes from. He is made even more uneasy by the silence of Jesus, and reminds Him that he has the power to crucify him or to set Him free. Our Lord replies, "Thou shouldst not have any power against me, unless it were given thee from above. Therefore he that hath delivered me to thee hath the greater sin" (JOHN 19:11), and Pilate is completely undone. In that shattering moment of truth, with the eyes of Our Lord upon him Pilate seeks above all to escape the dreadful predicament he finds himself in. But the roar of the crowd overwhelms him once more, and the punishment of Caesar seems more real than the injustice he is about to inflict on Christ; he succumbs to the rule of the mob.

In one final futile jibe at the crowd, Pilate asks them if he should crucify their King. In a deafening shout, the mob rejects the kingship of Christ and He is led away.

4. *The Carrying of the Cross*

Then therefore he delivered him to them to be crucified. And they took Jesus and led him forth. And bearing his own cross, he went forth to that place which is called Calvary, but in Hebrew Golgotha;" (JOHN 19:16-17).

What then had changed the peaceful rejoicing crowd of Palm Sunday, with their joyful chant of "Hosannah" into the vengeful crowd with its roar of "crucify Him" in the space of one week?

To all intents and purposes, it was a democratic choice, the choice of the people to bludgeon vacillating authority at the cost of the innocent. Public opinion, that universal misnomer for it often means nothing of the sort, and propaganda had been at work. The Chief Priests and the Pharisees, aware that their grip of events was threatened, moved into action and their emissaries went from house to house spreading deceit and inciting hatred. And within a week a peaceful people is turned into a howling mob.

And now, the inhabitants who had hailed Him only a week before, disowned Him and according to the Law of Liviticus, He was led from the city walls to the place of Crucifixion.

The procession was made up of officials, the centurion with his detachment of soldiers, the two thieves and Our Lord, making their way through a silent crowd, silent at last, apart from the few jeers still to be heard from stragglers hurrying to catch up, fearful of missing a moment of the excitement.

The cross that was roughly thrust onto the torn and bleeding shoulders of Christ weighed, we are told, nearly 200 pounds and was made from rough pine so that no doubt great splinters tore into His shoulder as He moved forward. Isaias had already foretold that "His government would be on his shoulder" and Our Lord Himself had spoken of it long before; "And he that taketh not up his cross and followeth Me, is not worthy of Me" (MT. 10:38) and again "Jesus said to his disciples: "If any man will come after me let him deny himself, and take up his cross and follow me. For he that will save his life will lose it; and he that shall lose his life for my sake shall find it." (MT. 16:24). The way of the Cross is the great lesson that our path to heaven is made up of one small step at a time in patience and self-denial, following the road to calvary as closely as our weak natures will allow.

Fearful once more, not that Jesus should suffer, but that as He fell yet again under the weight of the Cross He might die before reaching Calvary, the soldiers looked around for someone to carry the Cross, for the task was too demeaning for either a Jew or a soldier to undertake.

Their eyes fell on a pagan amongst the crowd, one Simon of Cyrene, unknown until now, but remembered for all time for this one brief moment. He was probably unwilling at first to be pulled into the drama but rose to the occasion and willingly took up his burden. Some who have suffering thrust upon them accept it with resignation and even joy, as the means of salvation. Simon of Cyrene must have been just such a one, for we learn from St. Paul that his sons, influenced by the action of their father, became pillars of the Church.

He was not the only one in that hostile crowd to be moved to pity for Our Lord. Throughout the story of the trial of Our Lord, most of his disciples and friends seem to have vanished with undignified haste.

No women appear to have been amongst those who called for His blood; the only woman who makes an appearance was the wife of Pilate who so urgently begged him to have nothing to do with Our Lord. Now Veronica bravely made her way through the crowd to wipe the dirt and blood from the face of Jesus with a linen cloth. How brave and certain her love, to elbow her way through that angry mob, probably pushing and shoving her and jeering at her courage.

And the women of Jerusalem weep in pity. Jesus stops and for the first time since the trial, breaks His silence. At a time when He might have been overwhelmed with grief and suffering, He speaks words of comfort and concern for them. "Daughters of Jerusalem, weep not over me; but weep for yourselves and for your children. For, behold, the days shall come, wherein they will say; Blessed are the barren and the wombs that have not born and the paps that have not given suck. Then shall they begin to say to the mountains; fall upon us, and to the hills; cover us. For if in the green wood they do these things, what shall be done in the dry?" (LUKE 23:28-31)

He was the "green wood" the tree of life; the dry wood was the doomed city of Jerusalem, and later the world which would be deaf to His word. Having spoken these words, He went on His way until the hill of Calvary was reached.

5. The Crucifixion

And it was almost the sixth hour: and there was darkness over all the earth until the ninth hour. And the sun was darkened and the veil of the temple was rent in the midst. And Jesus, crying with a loud voice, said: Father, into thy hands I commend my spirit. And saying this he gave up the ghost. Now, the centurion seeing what was done, glorified God, saying: "Indeed this was a just man.(LUKE 23:44-47)

Death means ultimately the punishment of sin. Until the sin of Adam, death had no place in God's plan. Until the sting of death was drawn there was little hope for mankind. As Jesus arrived at Calvary, the gruesome act of sacrifice entered its final stage.

Having roughly torn the clothes from the lacerated Body of Christ, the soldiers prepared to nail His limbs to the arms of the Cross. The precise positioning of the nails was a carefully worked out means of inflicting the greatest pain, at the same time ensuring that the hands were not literally torn from the arms. Their fearful work done, the last hammer blow echoing around the city walls beneath, the Cross was lifted and placed in the pit prepared for it, and the extended pinioned limbs of Jesus took His full weight as He hung before the soldiers, who were by now exhausted from their cruel task.

Those who were crucified would sometimes, in their excruciating pain, shout down foul abuse from mouths twisted in pain, to those who passed by. In His agony, Our Lord's concern was for His persecutors, "Father forgive them for they know not what they do." Forgive them? For torturing and murduring their Lord and Creator? *But*, that small yet saving let-out, they did not know what they were doing. In ignorance, their sin was redeemable, like that of Pilate before them; how different if they had been taught understanding, then how grevious would be their sin. And while this scene unfolded, the people remained, fascinated, as any human tragedy will always, unaccountably, attract the curious. "And they stood and watched Him," says St. Matthew, and the other evangelists make the same calm and yet reproachful observation in otherwise dramatic accounts of the event.

Egged on by the wrapt attention of the crowd, the soldiers and officials taunted Him, urging Him to prove He was God by coming down from the Cross and saving Himself. To accept the challenge Jesus could have come down from the Cross, restored to healthy manhood. But all that took place was foretold; He came to earth to take man to Paradise. If He had saved Himself, we would have remained unsaved. His sacrifice was for the salvation of man, promised from the time of the Fall. In the bleak Garden of Calvary the debt was paid.

On either side of Jesus there were crucified the two thieves. The first one seemed like many criminals before him and he cursed his fate and swore at the onlookers. His punishment was to be expected from the law of the time. The second thief understood this and said as much. "And he said to Jesus: Lord remember me when thou shalt come into thy Kingdom. And Jesus said to him: Amen, I say to thee; This day thou shalt be with me in paradise." (LUKE 23:42-43) How strange to think that Our Lord was first followed to Paradise by a condemned thief, for he was the first to receive the fruits of Calvary.

Shortly to follow was the centurion who had supervised the fulfillment of the verdict. He of all people present in authority and importance before his soldiers, seems the most unlikely candidate, but Our Lord chooses those least obvious to worldly values.

After three hours of agony Our Lord was near to death, while silhouetted against a darkening sky were the figures of John the Beloved disciple and Mary, His mother, standing bowed in grief at the foot of the Cross.

What must have been their thoughts? The disciples had fled and were hiding in the shadows of the city. Only Our Lady and St. John remained. They cannot fully have understood what was happening. They saw only that their beloved was hanging bleeding and dying before them and it is not difficult to imagine their torture of mind. Mary had known from the beginning that a sword would pierce her heart, but no warning could have prepared her for this. In the gathering gloom, they must have heard the voice of Jesus coming down to them deep and true, unbroken by pain. "When Jesus therefore had seen his mother and the disciple standing, whom He loved, he saith to his mother: Woman, behold thy son." (JOHN 19:26) by addressing Our Lady as "Woman" Jesus was reminding us of the words of Genesis. She was that woman, and He was her seed. Only through her fiat, or acceptance of the angel's message was God's plan carried out; she was His partner in Redemption.

How can we deny His dying command that we should honour His grieving Mother? And He made us the astonishing gift of making her our heavenly mother, in His words to St. John "Son, behold thy mother". Who could carry our imperfect prayers more perfectly to her Son, whose dying concern was for her? The prayer of the rosary bring us close to Calvary, to stand silently by those two figures at the foot of the Cross. It brings her comfort, for we are with her in keeping vigil with her beloved Son. "And bowing His head, He gave up the ghost." (JOHN 19:30)

THE GLORIOUS MYSTERIES

1. *The Resurrection*

And when the Sabbath was past, Mary Magdalen and Mary the mother of James and Salome bought sweet spices, that coming they might anoint Jesus. And very early in the morning, the first day of the week, they came to the sepulchre, the sun being now risen. And they said to one another; Who shall roll back the stone from the door of the sepulchre? And, looking into the sepulchre, they saw a young man sitting on the right side, clothed with a white robe; and they were astonished. Who said to them: be not frightened. You seek Jesus of Nazareth, who was crucified. He is risen; he is not here. Behold the place where thy laid him. But go, tell his disciples and Peter that he goeth before you into Galilee. Therefore you shall see him, as he told you. (MARK 16,1:7)

The night friends of Jesus now take their honoured place in history. Joseph of Arimathea had been to Pilate to ask for the Body of Christ, and together with Nicodemus and a few devoted followers, they prepared to take Our Lord down from the Cross. Mary must have been present, as they carefully lifted the torn limbs from the grasp of the nails, and removed the thorns from His brow, before they placed Him in her arms. How different the feelings of the young mother who smiled down at her Child so many years before, from the thoughts of the woman who, now in anguish, held the white and ravished body of her Son. And they annointed the Body with myrrh and spices and wrapped it carefully in white linen. St. John says "Now there was in the place where he was crucified a garden; and in the garden a new sepulchre, wherein no man yet had been laid". And there they laid Him, rolling a large stone across the entrance before vanishing into the night and obscurity.

What can have been the thoughts of the disciples? They had fled from the scene before the trial of Our Lord and nothing had been heard of them since then. They were cowering in fear, heartbroken at the turn of events, completely forgetting in their panic, that on many occasions they had been warned of what lay ahead, and that Our Lord had told them that on the third day He would rise again.

How often we doubt the promises of Christ. We feel, apart from anything else, that we are not up to much and certainly do not merit the future he holds out to us, and so we turn away. It is quite true that no one can ever deserve the Redemption, but we reject the Crucifixion if we fail to take literally the words of Christ.

The fact is that none of the disciples believed Our Lord; ironically it appears that the only ones to place any faith in His words were the Chief Priests and Scribes, for they hurriedly dispatched soldiers to mount guard on the tomb. They even set a time limit of three days on the guard, revealing their fear of the words of Christ, "I will destroy this temple made with hands, and within three days I will build another not made with hands." (MARK 14:58) The fact that they fully believed in some confused way that only the theft of the Body by the disciples could enable this promise to be fulfilled is no more farfetched than anything else they undertook.

Even Mary Magdalen and Mary the mother of James, who came sadly to the tomb at dawn on the morning after the Sabbath, came merely to embalm the body, to seek consolation in their grief. And before their astonished eyes, there appeared an angel seated beside the stone, now rolled away, saying just as the angel at the Annunciation, and at Lourdes and Fatima, "fear not". He told them the astounding news that He was risen, and was on His way to Galilee, and, with that wonderful concern of heaven for the faint, but loving, hearted, "going quickly, tell ye his disciples that he is risen". When they joyfully meet Our Lord, He too urges them to hurry and tell the disciples. Even in their pathetic fear and loss of courage Our Lord seeks to reassure them.

And still they cannot believe it. "And these words seemed to them as idle tales; and they did not believe them" (LUKE 24:11). While two of the disciples walk to Emmaus, they are so preoccupied with grief that they fail to recognize the Figure who falls into step beside them. In reply to His gentle question, they become voluble and chatter on about the depth of their misery, incapable of hearing or understanding even the long list of prophecies foretelling all that had taken place with which the Stranger rebukes them.

It is only when Our Lord broke bread with them that we are told "And their eyes were opened; and they knew him". St. Thomas even needed to plunge his fingers into the wounded hands before he could accept the risen Christ.

It is a small consolation to our wavering faith that even those who knew Him failed so miserably. But if they had believed more readily perhaps we would have found it more difficult. "Their infirmity" says St. Gregory, "was, if I may so put it, our future firmness."

The whole argument of our faith rests on this mystery. St. Paul said that if it is not a fact that Christ rose from the dead, then our faith is in vain. The feast of Easter is the greatest feast of the Church's year, and as the lumen Christi, the Easter candle, springs into life, we celebrate a rebirth and promise of resurrection for each and every one of His creation. For "He rose again, according to the Scriptures."

2. The Ascension

And it came to pass, whilst he blessed them, he departed from them and was carried up to heaven. (LUKE 24:51)

The mystery of the Ascension always seems to carry an air of sadness. The disciples had only just begun to understand the reality of the Resurrection, and the joy of the presence of Jesus in their midst must have been overwhelming. And yet He left them once more, and although they had been warned, they were consistent in this one respect for they failed to understand the words Our Lord spoke to them and remained happy to be with Him. How achingly sad they must have been when before their eyes, "whilst He blessed them, He departed from them and was carried up to Heaven". They stood gaping in such stark attention that an angel said to them "Ye men of Galilee, why stand you looking up to Heaven? this Jesus who is taken up from you into heaven shall so come as you have seen him going to heaven." And then they must have come to their senses, for St. Luke takes up the story, "And they adoring, went back into Jerusalem with great joy." (24:52) Why should they be so full of joy on this occasion when only forty days before they had run for cover when Our Lord left them for the first time? Something tremendous had happened in those forty days.

"Go and tell Peter" the angel at the sepulchre had told the two Marys. Peter, who some twenty-four hours earlier had denied any knowledge of Jesus. It was Peter who ran all the way to the sepulchre unable to believe or understand the words of Mary Magdalen, hardly daring to hope as he stared at the empty shroud. Dear, marvellous impetuous St. Peter who was so astonished to see Our Lord when He appeared by the lake at Galilee that he promptly fell out of the boat in his great joy. And when he had finally recovered himself and Our Lord asked him if he loved Him, St. Peter was mystified that He should even ask. He had never wavered in his love from the first moment when Our Lord had asked him who they said He was. On that occasion Our Lord had said "Thou art Peter and upon this rock I shall build my Church. And the gates of Hell shall not prevail against it." St. Peter seems to have made a muddle of most things since then; he so loved Jesus that he tried to dissuade Him from the Cross, because he loved Him. And when Our Lord asked him to watch with Him in the Garden of Olives, Peter fell fast asleep. And yet the angel was quite specific that it was Peter who was to be told.

Our Lord first appeared to a woman who had sinned, and Peter who had denied Him, but they had both repented. We have only to think of that look Our Lord gave St. Peter after his third denial to realize how bitterly St. Peter wept.

Upon that rock the Church was founded and St. Peter was to die the same death as his Lord, only he insisted that he was unworthy of such honour, and was crucified upside down instead.

"And Jesus, coming, spoke to them saying: all power is given to me in heaven and in earth. Go, therefore teach ye all nations; baptising them in the name of the Father and of the Son and of the Holy Spirit. Teaching them to observe all things whatsoever I have commanded you. And, behold, I am with you all days, even to the consummation of the world." (MT. 28:18-20)

3. *The Descent of the Holy Ghost*

And when the days of the Pentecost were accomplished they were all together in one place. And suddenly there came a sound from heaven, as of a mighty wind coming; and it filled the whole house where they were sitting. And there appeared to them parted tongues, as it were of fire; and it sat upon every one of them. And they were filled with the Holy Ghost; and they began to speak with divers tongues, according as the Holy Ghost have them to speak. (ACTS 2:1-4)

From the moment of the Resurrection, Jesus had prepared the disciples for the work that lay ahead. At first calming their fears and their disbelief, and then teaching them as their awakening understanding transformed them beyond recognition. "Then he opened their understanding, that they might understand the scriptures." (LUKE 24:45)

The city of Jerusalem was thronging with crowds drawn by the harvest festival when the disciples with Mary and the holy women gathered together in prayer to await the promised Coming.

When the sign was granted at Fatima in 1917 that Our Lady had promised the crowds that gathered were rewarded by the sight of the sun spinning in the sky until the earth seemed

covered in sheets of light; the effect of Pentecost was equally astonishing. For a gale suddenly arose around the building, and the
crowds gathered in Jerusalem came running from all directions to
see light in the form of flames hovering over the heads of the
disciples. Even more astonishing was the ease with which the disciples then spoke to each and every man in his own language, for
they had come from different areas and spoke in many different
dialects. At first the crowd accused them of being drunk, but St.
Peter rose to rebuke them. There was no uncertainty about him
now as he assumed his role as Christ's Vicar on earth, and there
was no hesitation as he spoke to them. When they had heard him
out, those same men who had sneered at the disciples only
minutes before, became the first fruits of the Holy Spirit. "What
shall we do" they asked St. Peter and he preached penance to
them and baptised, we are told, about three thousand souls.

Through His special gifts the Holy Spirit inspires and guides
the Church and all its member, if we will allow Him. No one
person can change the will of another, it may be influenced and
cajoled but never forcefully changed. The millions spent on the so
called hidden persuasion of advertising, and the eery workings of
the psychiatric wards are a measure of the effort required to attempt the impossible. God alone can change our wills through
the workings of the Holy Spirit, who abides in the soul from the
moment of Baptism, and unless we forcibly eject Him through
sin, he remains always there. We should listen to that voice
carefully. Sometimes it seems as though we only achieve one
small step at a time, and then utter darkness engulfs us. But the
gifts of the Holy Spirit are there for the asking, and give us a true
sense of proportion.

Through wisdom, we see the world for what it is; we could almost say that whereas the other gifts of the Holy Spirit, Understanding and Knowledge, enable us to look to heaven from earth,
with Wisdom we look upon earth from heaven, through the eyes
of grace.

4. *The Assumption of Our Lady*

Very little if anything, is known of the years that remained to Our Lady after the death and Resurrection of her Son. We know that she was with the disciples at Pentecost, and tradition has it that she lived until the age of sixty-three. She lived peacefully amongst the disciples and we can be certain that she prayed for the young Church.

We are left in complete ignorance of any words she may have spoken, for her words throughout her life were only recorded on seven occasions. The last reported words spoken by Mary were uttered at the Marriage Feast at Cana, when having responded to the need of the parents by speaking to her Son, Our Lady said: "Whatsoever He shall say to you, do ye" (JOHN 2:5) Throughout the entire New Testament, this is the only command Our Lady ever gives. Her love for her Son and her loving concern for His creatures, the knowledge that only by doing His will can we be truly content, both underline her eternal role as mediatrix. It told us everything we need to know, and no further words are ever recorded.

As a human being, Our Lady was bound by the rules of nature, and death is part of that rule. As the one creature born without original sin, and remaining without sin, there was nothing to retain her in the grave; Satan held no sway whatsoever over this Immaculate personage.

There is a painting in Florence which portrays a tomb, supposedly that of Our Lady, but it is empty and all that emerges from its cavernous depth are cascades of roses. A sentimental but nevertheless apt metaphor for the Assumption of Our Lady from her earthly death.

This is the traditional teaching of the Church. Nowadays, tradition has a quaintly folksy image, but to the Church it means that teaching which is handed down from the Apostles, from one memory to the next, in one unceasing chain. The traditional teaching of the Assumption has long been accepted and was the subject of meditation in the prayer of the rosary from the thirteenth-century, long before the final seal of Papal approval in the twentieth-century.

The Assumption forms the second part of the promise to mankind. For Our Lady had to die, but she was assumed body and soul into heaven as we shall be. For her there was no shadow of death, for her sinless state freed her from the grave immediately. We must await the Final Day, but we have the evidence of the Assumption to fill us with optimism and hope.

5. *The Coronation of Our Lady in Heaven*

How wonderful must have been that meeting between the Son and His mother. The Son who had been born in a cave, and had lived subject to her, and the mother who had never protested at the agonizing betrayal and death that had taken place before her grief stricken eyes, for she understood God's love for man and His plan for our redemption.

Even more wondrous to meditate is the meeting between God and the one creature who so perfectly responded to His grace, that she became the new Eve, the perfection of His creation to restore all that had been lost in the Garden of Eden when the human race began its long straggling march to Calvary.

Perfection is almost impossible for most of us to imagine. So far is it from our comprehension, that in any agony of discomfort, we have manoeuvered the meaning to something more bearable and material, trivialising its real meaning. In the same way the word "divine" has been casually misplaced without understanding. But perhaps it is not totally crass for somewhere in the back of our minds we know that the ultimate is divine and perfect, only we have momentarily forgotten what it means.

The angel Gabriel told us at the Annunciation that Mary was full of grace, and so completely in favour with God, that perhaps Mary was the only true comtemplative who never had need to place any obstacle between herself and the world in order to speak with God. How often we think that all we need is to find some peaceful oasis in order to escape the muddles that surround us. We should meditate on the life of Our Lady which was so ordinary and full of humility that no one ever thought of mentioning her again. Certainly she was never mentioned for herself, but only in relation to the actions of her Son.

As the mother of God, she was the most important woman in the world there has ever been or ever will be, but no one seems to have noticed. Although there were paintings on the walls of the catacombs showing Our Lady carrying the Child Jesus, it was not until her own glory was necessary for that of her Son that the early Christians gradually became aware of her. In the fourth-century, the Church taught the virginity of Mary in answer to those who denied the humanity of Christ. From then on devotion to Our Lady grew, and in the General Council held at Epheus in 431, the term "Mother of God" was decreed. From Our Lady herself all was silence and humility.

Fra Angelico was so enamoured of the intimacy of the scene of the Coronation of Our Lady, that unlike his other paintings of heaven which show celestial scenes of the Blessed stepping, almost dancing, through a garden of trailing flowers, while the hordes of the damned curse their fate in terrible agony, in the Coronation of Our Lady, all is banished.

Our Lord gently and tenderly places the crown on His mother's bowed head. It is an image of inexpressible love. The only people to witness this intimate scene are the saints beneath, for Our Lady is nearer to God than all the hosts of angels and saints . . . and yet she is the most holy mother of each and everyone of us, and to us she has given her crown of the rosary. The future is in our own hands, and how little we have to fear if within those hands are held the beads of the rosary.

Selection of Primary Sources

Garden Craft in the Bible: Eleanor Sinclair Rhode. Herbert Jenkins. London, 1927.

The Garden: Julia Burrell. Thames & Hudson, 1966.

Mediaeval Gardens: John Harvey. B. T. Batsford Ltd. London, 1981.

Mediaeval English Gardens: Theresa McLean. Collins. London, 1981.

The Splendour of the Rosary: Maisie Ward. Sheed & Ward, 1946.

Our Lady's Dowry: Father Bridgett. Burns & Oates Ltd. London, 1894.

Monastic Order in England: David Knowles. Cambridge University Press, 1940.

The Secret of the Rosary: St. Louis de Montfort. Montfort Publication, New York, 1965.

Legends of the Madonna: Mrs. Jameson. Longmans & Green & Co., 1909.

The Rose Garden Game: Eithne Wilkins. Victor Gollancz Ltd., London, 1969.

Pietas Mariana Britannica: Waterton St. Joseph's Catholic Library, 1879.

The Nun's Rule Being the Ancren Riwle: Modernised by James Morton. Introduction by Abbot Gasquet. Alexandra Moring Ltd. De la More Press, London, 1905.

St. Aelred of Rivaulx: T. Edmund Harvey. H. R. Allenson Ltd., 1932.

Shrines of England & Wales: H .M. Gillett. Samuel Walker Ltd., 1957.

Series on the Rosary: Father Thurston in the *Month Magazine,* 1900.

The Great Heresies: Hilaire Belloc. Sheed & Ward, London, 1938.

A History of Jewellery 1100-1870: Joan Evans. Faber & Faber, London.

Edmund Campion: Evelyn Waugh. Oxford University Press, 1980.

The Crusades: Stephen Runciman. C.U.P., 1951.

The Great Siege—Malta 1565: Ernle Bradford. Hodder & Stoughton, London, 1961.

Philip II: William Thomas Walsh. Sheed & Ward, London, 1938.

St. Pius V: Robin Anderson. Tan Books, Illinois, 1978.

This Apocalyptic Age: Robert Bergin. Voice of Fatima International 1970.

The Rosary in Action: John S. Johnson. Tan Books, 1954.

By the Queen's Command: Lawrence F. Harvey. John Burns & Sons, Glasgow, 1951.

The Happy Grotto: Fulton Ousler. The World's Work: Surrey, 1913.

Bernadette of Lourdes: Francis Parkinson Keyes, 1953.

The Life of Christ: Fulton J. Sheen. Pan Books. London, 1959.

Pastoral Sermons: Ronald Knox. Burns & Oates. London, 1960.

Notes

CHAPTER ONE

1. Genesis Chap. 2:8.
2. Genesis Chap. 3:8.
3. Isaiah Chap. 58:11.
4. Song of Solomon Chap. 4:12.
5. *The Garden*, Julia Berrell. Thames & Hudson, 1966. p. 96.
6. Museum: Frankfurt Am Main.
7. Museum Verona.
8. Maisie Ward: *The Splendour of the Rosary*. Sheed & Ward, London, 1946.
9. Solomon's Song, Chap. 2:i.
10. *Garden Craft in the Bible*: Eleanor Sinclair Rhode. London, 1927.
11. *Butler's Lives of the Saints*. London and Dublin, 1954.
12. *The Garden*: Julia Berrell. Thames & Hudson, 1966, p. 92.
13. *Mediaeval Gardens*: Theresa McLean. Collins, 1981.

CHAPTER TWO

1. *Pietas Mariana Britannica*. London 1879. Watterton. p. 43.
2. Sermon 20: *Migne Patrilogia. Tom cvcv col.* 522-24.
3. The Annunciation had been celebrated in England since the fifth-century, and was known here as "Lady-day". The term is still in use today.
4. *The Nun's Rule Being the Ancren Riwle*. Modernised by James Morton with Introduction by Abbot Gasquet. Alexander Moring Ltd., London, 1905.
5. *Speculum Ecclesiae* Cap xxii: Bib Max Tom xxv.
6. *The Mirror of Our Lady* written in 1430 — Early English Text Society 1873.
7. *Our Lady's Dowry*: Father T. Bridgett p. 188.
8. *The Splendour of the Rosary*: Maisie Ward. Sheed & Ward, 1946, p. 42.
9. Related by Father Bede Jarrett.
10. *Pietas Mariana Britannica*: Waterton Book the Second Page 10.
11. *The Month*, 1900.
12. Luke ii-19.
13. *The Month*. December, 1900. Fr. Thurston.
14. "A Relation of the Island of England". Printed for the Cambden Society. *Our Lady's Dowry* by Fr. Bridgett.

CHAPTER FOUR

1. *Our Lady's Dowry*, Father Bridgett.
2. TESTAM. Ebor. Vol. IV p. 257 (Surtees Society, 1868).

3. *Testamenta Vestuta.* Sir H. Nicholas, p. 141.

4. *Testamenta Eboracensia.* Vol. IV, p. 231 (Surtees 1868).

5. *Testamenta Eboracensia.* Vol. IV p. 231 (Surtees 1868).

6. *Testamenta Eboracensia.* Vo. IV p. 27 (Surtees 1868).

7. *Testamenta Vestuta.* Sir H. Nicholas, p. 141.

8. *A History of Jewellery 1100-1870.* Joan Evans. Faber & Faber. p. 77.

9. IBID.

10. Prologue n.iii.

11. Sir Thomas More: *Dialogue of Comfort* Ch. xiv.

12. *The Rose Garden Game*: Ethne Wilkins. Victor Gollancz Ltd. 1969, p. 49.

·

CHAPTER SIX

1. *The Apocalyptic Age.* Robert Bergin. Voice of Fatima International 19, p. 11.

2. *The Queen's Command.* Lawrence Harvey, p. 33. John S. Burns & Son, Glasgow, 1979.